The Case of the Whispering Well

The Feline Files - Book 1

K.E. O'Connor

K.E. O'Connor Books

PRINT ISBN: 978-1-915378-95-8

THE CASE OF THE WHISPERING WELL

Chapter 1

The ancient snow globe shimmered on the desk, its silver flakes swirling in slow, lazy circles. I pressed my booping snooter close to the glass until the chill made my whiskers twitch.

"Sage? Are you there?" My voice sounded too loud in the musty stillness of the library. "I need to tell you something."

Ever since I'd been trapped in Badger's Haze, I'd searched for a way to contact home. It took a while and lots of cursing, the non-magical kind, but with help from Sage, we'd forced a connection with Crimson Cove using this unreliable globe. It sometimes worked when it had a mind to.

The swirling mist inside the globe pulled together, revealing the familiar scowl of my best friend. Sage looked like I'd woken her from the deepest, most satisfying nap of her life. Her ears were flattened, and her fur stuck up along one side of her body.

"It's three in the morning! Some of us actually sleep at night," she grumbled.

"Sleep is for cats without a purpose."

Her eyes narrowed. "When exactly did you find one of those? You've been moping ever since we set up this connection."

I gave the library's dusty shadows a pointed look. My prison. My exile. "Wouldn't you, in my situation? Anyway, that's not important. I found something in the basement."

Sage groaned. "Let me guess... another mouse skeleton?"

"Much more interesting."

"A witch's skeleton? Nothing would surprise me about Badger's Haze. That place is yucky."

"No! It's boxes of Angel Force paperwork. Old, unsolved murders."

Sage yawned so wide I could see every stubby, blunt tooth. "And?"

"This is why Angel Force sent me here."

"To meddle?" she asked. "After everything that happened in Crimson Cove? You must have learned your lesson by now."

"I didn't meddle. I helped!" I tried to sound dignified, although the memory of my unfair banishment still made my ears burn with shame. "I have to show Angel Force how valuable I am. These unsolved murders happened right here in Badger's Haze, and the angels abandoned them. You know what that means."

"I do not know, and I don't want to know."

"It means they banished me here so I can solve them."

Sage snorted. "Or they banished you because you're a menace who almost blew up Crimson Cove."

2

"I'm innocent. You know that, don't you?"

Sage's long sigh fogged the snow globe. "I do. This place isn't the same without you. It's lovely and quiet. And Cythera hasn't pulled a single feather out in weeks."

"Her anxiety feather plucking has nothing to do with me." I pulled the nearest file toward me, brushing off a fine layer of dust that made my booping snooter itch. "These cold cases need my help."

Sage shook her head. "Don't do it. You'll get in trouble. And you've no backup if you find yourself in a mess."

"A higher power has called on my super-sleuth skills."

"If you've already decided, why wake me up at this ridiculous hour?"

"Because, as you so smartly pointed out, I have no support and barely any magic. I need your help. Eliza Thorny. Does that name ring any bells?"

Her gaze went distant. "Nope."

"Get researching. Back in the day, her murder made the front pages. There are clippings in the file. Eliza wasn't just any witch. Her lineage had serious power. Fire magic."

"Thorny and fire magic. That does sound familiar. But being half asleep puts me at a disadvantage. Can't this wait until the morning and after I've had my third breakfast?"

"No. Let me jog your memory, then you can look through anything useful in Vorana's bookstore."

"Juno!"

"It'll take five minutes."

"You won't stop pestering until I'm fully awake, will you?"

"You know I make your life more interesting."

"More stressful." Sage settled with her front paws tucked underneath her. "Go on."

"Eliza was an elemental witch found dead beside an ancient magical well in Badger's Haze. The well was important. People made pilgrimages there before this village went bad."

"Hmmm. Interesting. There are only a few enchanted wells left," Sage said. "They keep being drained or destroyed when the magic sours. Old magic often curdles. You'd know all about that."

"This well is famous. Supposedly, it whispers to people. I need more information, though, so see what you can dig up."

"Doesn't your library have everything you need?"

"It's not my library, just a temporary base," I said. "And most of the books have mildew or water damage. I'll keep looking, but backup is required. From the case notes I've read so far, Eliza's death was odd. She was found beside the well with ritual items scattered around her, and her body was crystallized from the inside."

"That's... unsettling." Sage shuddered. "But why do you care?"

"Because I'm trapped in this miserable place with nothing to do but chase mice, sneeze over dusty books, and miss Zandra. This is a test. If I solve it, the angels will let me come home to Crimson Cove."

Sage snorted. "Angel Force isn't clever enough to set tests like that."

"Harsh but fair. So, I show them how much they need me. I was their expert consultant. A somebody."

"You're still a somebody," Sage said, "just one with terrible judgment who can't keep her mouth shut and her magic under control."

"I speak my mind. And... well, yes, the magic can be unhinged." I flopped onto my belly. "Help me fix this mess. It hurts to be apart from Zandra. Everything aches. My heart most of all."

Sage wrinkled her nose. "If you must do this, pick another case. That well sounds like bad news. If it didn't stop the murder of a powerful witch happening right beside it, then the magic is broken. It's bad, old, messed-up magic."

Sage's insight was as welcome as it was irritating. "I'm investigating. And you're helping. Any advice, old friend?"

"Don't do it."

"That's not an option."

"Then go at noon when the sun is strongest. Moonlight and water are a powerful combination. And for cat's sake, don't drink the water."

"I knew you cared."

"I care about not having to explain to Zandra why her exiled familiar drowned in a magical well that summons death."

"I'll report back. In the meantime, sneak down to Vorana's bookstore and find me everything you can on the Badger's Haze whispering well. I need a potted history so we can connect the dots."

"There is no *we*. You're on your own."

"Where's the fun in that? Since those foolish higher angels forced me out of Crimson Cove, you've been bored."

"Boredom is the safe option," Sage said. "And I like not facing death on a regular basis."

"Safe is dull. And you've still got some of my magic, you fortunate thing. That means you can take risks without worrying about the consequences. Admit it. You're bored and you miss me."

"Safe won't get me exiled. My witch will always have me by her side."

Those words hit like a fist to the gut. "Lucky you."

Sage closed her eyes for a second. "If I could find an emoji for a sigh and a hug, I'd send a hundred. I'll read the dumb books in the morning, but that's all. And we need to be careful. If I'm caught talking to an exiled criminal, I'll get in trouble."

"I'm mistakenly exiled," I corrected. "And you have the globe under the shelf in Vorana's office, don't you?"

"Sure. Although it was tricky to move out of the living room. Vorana keeps asking me if I've seen it. I hate deceiving her."

"It's for her own good. The fewer people who know we're talking, the less risk there is." I leaned closer. "Thanks, Sage. I knew I could count on you. Message me later when you have news."

The silver flakes swirled one last time before Sage's face dissolved into mist. The globe went dark, and I was alone again, except for the library ghosts, the mice, and cold cases stacked around me, whispering for attention.

Chapter 2

By early afternoon, the library felt like it was swallowing me whole. The air was heavy with the scent of mildew and centuries-old parchment, and my whiskers kept twitching at the faint skitter of something alive in the stacks. I really hoped it was just mice.

I was considering whether to risk a nap on the least dusty pile of books when the snow globe shimmered to life on the desk.

Sage's scruffy face appeared through the swirl. She blinked at me with tired eyes. "Juno? You there? I've been reading all morning, and my eyes hurt."

"For me? You shouldn't have." I hopped onto the desk so I could see her.

"I did it for me. The sooner you have this information, the sooner you'll stop pestering me at all hours and risk me waking Vorana. And I'm old! Everything aches. I need my sleep."

"With my magnificent magic in your veins, you must feel half your actual age. How old is that exactly?"

"That's still old."

I snorted a laugh. "What did you learn about the whispering well?"

"As you said, it's ancient." Sage settled back as though preparing for a lecture. Her image wobbled slightly in the globe's mist, but her voice was steady. "It predates Badger's Haze, and that place was built over a thousand years ago. The village formed around the well. I couldn't find records of when it was dug, only that it's always been there."

"Someone must have built it."

"The first settlers considered it sacred. They called it the Eye of the Earth and believed it connected our world to other planes of existence. Worlds we have no business snooping into, full of primeval magic, danger, and mystery."

"We should be free to visit all magical realms," I said. "It's practically our duty."

She narrowed her eyes. "Yes, because that's never landed anyone in trouble before. Angel Force classified the well as a natural magical nexus."

"That's in a book?"

"No," Sage said. "That's from Vorana's notes in the margins. She studied nexus points. Some magic users call them anchor points."

"Your witch is delightfully bookish."

"Is that an insult?"

"I always recommend reading. I wish Zandra would take to books, but she never studies."

"She's powerful enough without learning more magic."

"Yes. She truly is. Witchy perfection in all forms. What else?"

"The water changes with the lunar cycle," Sage said. "A full moon turns it into a conduit for elemental magic. A new moon makes it..." She trailed off, frowning. "Unknown. A page is torn out."

I sat up straighter. "Inconvenient. Maybe deliberate? To hide knowledge?"

"Or just an ill-mannered customer who wanted the information but didn't want to pay for the whole book." Sage glanced over her shoulder. "I've got to go. Vorana's calling. It's snack time."

"Is it salmon?" I asked hopefully.

"Yes! I dreamed about catching one like the bears do. It was huge, and I ate it all myself."

"I miss Vorana's cooking. And Sorcha's salmon."

Sage's eyes went half-lidded in bliss. "Yeah, especially when she makes it with that butter rub after frying it in goose fat."

I gave a wistful sigh. "Before you stuff your face without sparing a thought for my ever-present hunger, I'll send you the case file summary on Eliza. I've read it a few times, but I don't want to miss anything. A second pair of eyes is welcome."

Sage's head tilted. "We can send stuff through this thing? We can't even get a stable image."

"I think so." I peered at the base of the globe. "Hang on, I'm still working out this old tech. If only Randal were here. He'd give me an upgrade." I tapped a paw on the glass and tentatively pressed the faded mark that I thought was a transmission link. "Let me know what comes through."

Her ears perked. "Wow! I got it! Give me time to read while I eat. I'll reconnect when I'm done."

The globe went dark, leaving me in the library hush once more.

Case File: #83-1104 – Badger's Haze
Homicide Department
Date Filed: November 16, 1999
Victim Information
Name: Thorny, Eliza Marie
Age: 42
Address: 17 Hemlock Lane, Badger's Haze
Occupation: Herbalist / Proprietor of Thorny Remedies
Magical Speciality: Elemental (fire)

Case Summary
The body was discovered on November 15, 1999, at 6:17 a.m. by Samuel Greene, caretaker of the Badger's Haze well. The victim was found lying face-up at the well's edge. There were no signs of a struggle or defensive wounds.
Cause of death: unexplained magic. Autopsy pending.

Scene Details:
Location: Badger's Haze Central Square
Weather: Clear, 38°F at dawn

Evidence Collected:

Glass vial (empty) with cork stopper, found 3 feet from the body
Chalk markings on well stones (photographed)
Red candle stub, partially melted
Silver pendant with fire symbol (victim's)
Trace herbs: rosemary, cinnamon, cloves
Well water sample (unstable properties – inconclusive tests)

Timeline – November 14–15, 1999:

9:00 a.m. Opened shop (witness: Iris Montgomery)
1:30 p.m. Closed shop early
2:15 p.m. Argument with Bartholomew Winters near the well
4:45 p.m. Purchased candles and chalk (receipt in pocket)
7:00 p.m. Globe conversation with Vera Blackling
10:30 p.m. Seen by neighbor leaving home
11:00 p.m.–6:17 a.m. No sightings until body discovery

Persons of Interest:

Bartholomew Winters (53): Local business owner, professional rivalry, argument at the well.

Englebert Turgleton (47): Landowner, proposed marriage one week prior (rejected), property overlooks crime scene.

Vera Blackling (27): Apprentice, argued with the victim, last known to speak with her.

Iris Montgomery (41): Close friend, beneficiary in will.

Samuel Greene (61): Well caretaker, discovered the body.

Zaren Trooli (44): Boyfriend, rumors of an argument.

There were signs of a search at the victim's home before the investigators arrived. Several books on elemental manipulation were left open on a desk.

Handwritten note: *The water in the well tested normal, but it felt wrong. Ever since this case landed on my desk, I've been having nightmares. This might be the case that makes me retire.* Officer Hogarth.

The list of suspects read like the cast list for a tragedy. A rejected suitor, an ambitious apprentice, and a friend who benefited from Eliza's murder. And then there was the argumentative boyfriend, the well caretaker who found the body, and a missing grimoire.

But it was Officer Angel Hogarth's scrawl that had my fur standing on end. The water felt *wrong*. I sat back, curling my tail around my paws. What lurked in that well? And did its murky depths hide secrets about what really happened to Eliza?

Chapter 3

The snow globe flickered to life, and Sage came into view, the flakes swirling around her like a miniature blizzard.

"Well?" I asked. "What did you make of that?"

"Well indeed," she said. "That magical pit sounds iffy. Should I tell you again to stay away, or have you already visited?"

I lifted my chin. "No. I listened to your wise advice. I need more information before dipping my paw into those murky waters. Especially now that I'm without any magic." My stomach growled. "How was the salmon?"

Sage's eyes gleamed. "Delicious. I had two servings."

I groaned. "Cruel. Anyway, the angels thought Eliza's death was foul play. There's a suspect list."

"I saw that," Sage said. "The books I read mention other deaths close to the well. They happened in 1891, 1924, 1957, and 1990. All powerful witches or magic practitioners. The angels were right to be suspicious. Eliza's death was no accident."

"All the deaths happened thirty-three years apart."

Sage narrowed her eyes. "I can do math, thank you. But a murder in 1999 doesn't fit the pattern."

"The other deaths are unrelated to Eliza's murder? Or maybe someone wanted Angel Force to think they were linked." I leaned closer to the globe. "The previous deaths might have been approved sacrifices to a water deity. Some of the old gods are bloodthirsty."

"Whoever killed Eliza tried to cover their tracks by making it look like they were appeasing a god," Sage said. "It's a shame they can't count. If they'd picked the right year, they might have got away with it."

"They have. But not for much longer," I muttered. "I went through the autopsy, and it's bizarre. Eliza's organs were crystallized, as if frozen from the inside out."

Sage winced. "That wouldn't have been a fun way to die."

"And the even weirder part? The ground around her had burn marks. A circle of scorched earth."

"Fire and ice," Sage said. "Opposing elements. Maybe there was a fight using those elements."

I nodded. "The magical residue left behind was off the charts. Angel Force couldn't measure it properly. Their magic kept misfiring, and the water samples came back void or corrupted."

"Incompetence or faulty equipment?" Sage asked.

I chuckled. "Don't let Cythera hear you say that. How is my fearsome angel friend?"

"I stay out of her way whenever I can."

"Does she still hate me?"

"She never hated you," Sage replied after a pause. "Well... maybe a little. Cythera was doing her job. The higher angels ordered your banishment, so that's what she did. You can't blame her for that."

"I don't. I saw regret in Cythera's eyes before she sent me here." I tapped a paw on the desk. "Let's focus. Eliza. The file mentions the suspects, but did you see that note about the well water feeling wrong from an angel investigating the crime scene?"

Sage tilted her head. "Sure. But what does that mean?"

"No idea. But he requested a transfer off the case. There's a note in the case file. I looked into him. He retired during the investigation and went off-grid. I can't find anything about him since 2000."

Sage grunted. "Those nightmares he mentioned must have been bad."

"Ask Finn if he can track down Angel Hogarth," I said. "Angel Force must keep a record of retirees."

"I'll see what I can do." Sage's ears twitched. "The book I've been reading says the well water has the power to destroy. It's unstable. Only a water witch can control it. That's who you should target. They've got to be involved in this murder."

A slow smile spread across my face. "And I have the perfect candidate. But before we get to that, I'm sending over Eliza's autopsy report."

Sage grimaced. "Is it gruesome?"

"It's factual. Just don't eat any salmon while reading." I fiddled with the globe's base until the faint hum of magic signaled the connection was active. "The report is whisking your way now. Let me know what you think."

Autopsy Report: County Morgana Medical Examiner's Office

Victim: Eliza Thorny
Date: November 23rd, 1999
Examiner: Angel Lydia, assisted by Angel Voss

Preliminary Notes:

Body identified via dental records. Female, age 42.
Estimated time of death: 5–8 hours before discovery.
Clothing intact but brittle, coated in crystal deposits (concentrated along the abdomen).

External Examination:

Height: 5 feet 4 inches
Weight: 168 lbs (estimated pre-crystallization; crystal deposits added 20 lbs)
Hair: Ash blonde, shoulder-length, loose braid.
Eyes: Open, pupils dilated. Irises show an opalescent sheen shifting between violet and blue. No known pathology. Ocular fluid solidified upon contact

with the needle.

No external trauma to the head or neck. No signs of asphyxiation or strangulation.

Silvery residue on fingertips and nails, glowing faintly under black light. Trace elements: quartz, hematite, and an unidentified compound emitting low-level electromagnetic pulses.

Faint circular burn on sternum, ringed with six pinprick holes.

Hairline fractures radiate from a burn site, filled with translucent, faintly glowing crystal veins in a symmetrical pattern

Internal Examination:

All major organs intact but fully crystallized.

No tissue decay or decomposition present.

Heart mass: 2.4 times expected weight. Composition: hybrid of quartz, beryl, and trace stibnite. Heart surface etched with ancient rune markings in a webbed pattern.

Lungs contained particles resembling snowflake obsidian.

No blood present. Vascular structures were hollow, lined with reflective crystal sheathing.

Brain transformed into a latticework

of amethyst filaments, hemispheric structure intact but inorganic.

Cause of Death: Magical transformation through systemic crystallization of internal structures, originating at the heart and spreading through circulatory and nervous systems. The symmetry and precision indicate a deliberate magical act, not an accident.

Additional Notes: Local legend describes the well as sentient. Historical accounts mention unexplained phenomena and ritual deaths every 33 years.

Report forwarded to the Occult Incidents Review Board. Body sealed under a warded lock pending further instructions.

I traced a paw over the rune diagram sketched in the margin, my claws snagging on the rough paper, and a shiver rippled through my fur. I knew magic like this. I'd once held it in my paws, the kind that could unmake or transform with a thought. Back then, it had been mine to command.

Eliza hadn't just been killed. She'd been changed, piece by piece. Whoever did this wanted their mark to last forever. Eliza's body was a testament to a terrifying power.

Did that power still lurk in this downtrodden little place? Or had the killer fled?

I might be weaker now, but I wasn't powerless. Whoever destroyed Eliza wasn't getting away with it. Not while I breathed.

Chapter 4

The snow globe lit up, Sage's fluffy whiskered face sharpening in the mist. Her eyes were wide. "I just finished reading. Nasty."

"At least they started with her heart. Eliza wouldn't have suffered. That's a small mercy," I said. "It's no wonder Angel Force never solved this case. They needed an expert to figure out what happened."

Sage's ears tipped forward. "You mean you. You think you can solve this murder after so much time has gone by?"

"I can solve anything. But instead of using my skills, the angels banished their best and brightest over a tiny snafu." I tilted my head. "Has Cythera mentioned how bad her key performance indicators are since I got thrown out of Crimson Cove?"

Sage huffed out a breath. "Let's not go there. What else have you got? Did the occult lot dig up anything useful? I'm guessing not, since they never cracked the case."

"I was getting to that." I leaned closer to the globe. "Are you ready? It's a huge file."

She snorted. "So long as your antique globe can handle the data. I've read a few of their publications. They waffle."

"The globe is smoking from the base, but I'll risk it. If you don't hear from me, send a rain cloud to Badger's Haze to put out the blaze. Paws crossed."

Her face flickered, fuzzing into static. "Nothing came through. Juno? You there?"

"Hold on. There's a small fire!" I swatted at the tendrils of smoke curling off the glass. "Hexes and haunts! The occult file had a magic lock on it and went poof when I tried to send it."

"Can you break it?"

"Not like I used to," I said, heat prickling my ears with embarrassment. "But I've kept up my daily practice of old-school magic. I'm learning something new every week. I'll figure out a workaround."

Sage's eyes narrowed. "I thought you gave up on potions after you singed off one side of your whiskers?"

"I've got the basics down. I'm determined to succeed." I flexed my murder mittens over the globe's base. "Give me another minute."

Sage yawned, a huge, jaw-cracking effort. "I could nap while you figure things out. All that snacking has made me sleepy."

"No snoozing when we have a case to crack. The glass hummed under my paws. Here we go. Still getting smoke, still stamping on flames, but you should get the information through in a second. Enjoy the read. And try not to fall asleep."

Occult Incidents Review Board – Department for Anomalous Mortality
File No: OIRB/99/NOV/447-E
Subject: Eliza Thorny (Deceased, Age 42)
Date of Report: December 18th, 1999

Summary: Following Angel Lydia's autopsy report, the OIRB conducted an examination of Eliza Thorny's body and the enchanted well in Badger's Haze.

Body Examination:

Crystallization consistent with Thaumafrost Event Type C. Organs replaced by a translucent crystalline lattice, composition unknown. Shards dissolved into vapor in sunlight.

Eyes transformed into mirrored rings reflecting unknown environments. Pattern matches the Seven-Spiral glyph from *Codex Rivenfall, Book of Doors*.

Residual whispering reported by three OIRB personnel who visited the well, repeating the phrase *between and beneath*.

Relevant Historical Cases – Badger's Haze Well:

BHW-1891-A — Agnes Merryweather (68): Hedge-witch and herbalist, known for speaking to the well she called the Listening Hollow.. Witnesses saw a blue glow circling her home the night before her death. She was found beside the well, hands submerged in water that had risen unnaturally high. Entire body drained of color. Veins and arteries dry. A spellbook open to *The Trade: Offer, Ask, Await.*

Conclusion: Attempted a pact with a sentient transplanar entity. The entity refused the trade and took payment, regardless. Classified *Fatal Rejection: Energy Drain.*

BHW-1924-D – Penelope Ashcroft (25): An alchemical scholar studying ley lines and memory wells. Identified the Badger's Haze well as a high-concentration echo site. Found seated against the stone, eyes fused shut with gold filament, fingertips glowing with circular symbols. Remained alive but mute for two hours before calcifying into marble.

Conclusion: Voluntary ritual attempt to anchor her essence in an echo dimension. Transformation indicates partial success.

Recommendations:

Immediate quarantine of the well. A stone seal and a permanent iron gate to be ordered.

Placement of warning glyphs in perimeter signage to dissuade non-sensitive locals or visitors to the village.

The snow globe shimmered, silver flakes swirling until Sage's face came into view.

"You read all of it?" I asked.

"I skimmed. I focused on the important bits. There are too many deaths linked to wells. We already know not to trust water, but this is ridiculous."

"Ponds, streams, lakes, the sea." I curled my lip. "It's all a giant toilet for fish. And don't get me started on what happens to the fluids when they mate. Yuck!"

"Yep. Unless it comes from a tap and Vorana encourages me in with treats and her scented oils, I steer clear of water."

"All those deaths, and Angel Force solved none of them," I said. "They're missing one crucial thing."

She gave me a flat look. "And what would that be?"

"An enchanting, magical talking familiar to run the show!"

"I wish I could find the snort-laugh emoji. And maybe one for a giant ego."

"I'm not bragging, just stating the obvious. I'm excellent at deciphering the facts. Something the angels on this case failed to do, since they never found the killer."

Sage gave a resigned nod. "I don't put much store in this report. The occult lot are fearmongers. Vorana hates it when they demand to check our shop's inventory. They're convinced she's hiding a stash of dark grimoires in some secret room. And they always eat the good cookies and leave the oatmeal and raisin for Vorana."

"In this case, they had a right to be nervous. I checked whether anyone followed through on their recommendations. The council rejected the quarantine order, and a year later, locals tore down the warning glyphs and fencing."

"You think someone paid the angels to look the other way? Or was this a cover-up?"

"More likely, it was their usual incompetence. Angels can't be bribed. Well, most of them can't. They won't get their golden halo at retirement if they're shady."

"You're grouchy," Sage said. "Have a nap. We can get back to it later."

"You sleep. I want to review more suspects."

"You know what happens when you don't nap."

"If I had Zandra to curl up with, I'd take my usual number of cozy naps. It's no fun to nap alone."

"You're asleep! You don't know if you're alone or surrounded by a gang of rabid rats."

"You know what I mean."

Sage's expression softened. "I do. Naps are better when Vorana's around. I like opening my eyes and she's the first thing I see. That, or snacks. Buzz me when you're ready to talk again."

The connection faded, and I yawned before hitting the reset button on the snow globe. Maybe a nap wouldn't be a bad thing. I just needed the right crunchy paper to settle on, and I'd catch forty winks.

Chapter 5

Sage's voice cut through my nap. Although I missed her words, I recognized her cranky tone. I opened my eyes to see her image sharpening in the globe.

"How's your mood?" she asked.

I rolled over and did a big stretch. "Improved. You were right. I needed a snooze."

"I knew it. And how's the globe?"

"Rebooted, not smoking, and kicked."

"Kicked?"

"I thumped it too just before dozing off. It's behaving, but I don't know how long it'll be before it bursts into flames again, so let's not waste time."

Sage's whiskers quivered in amusement. "Let's review what we've got. Eliza's death was horrible, caused by dark, powerful magic, and deliberate. Someone's behind it. Who's first on your list? And please tell me you've postponed your plan to go well diving."

"For now," I said. "But it's still on my itinerary."

"Shall I send you a snorkel and flippers?"

"I look forward to my gifts. Right, the suspects. We've got Bartholomew Winters. You read in the Angel Force report that he had a problem with

Eliza. He's an elemental witch specializing in water magic, while Eliza mastered the fire element. Their philosophies could have clashed."

"Do you have his interview?"

"Right here." I nudged the file toward the globe. "If only I had opposable thumbs, this would be so much quicker to send."

"If we had them, we'd rule the world and be unstoppable," Sage said.

I grinned. "I almost did once. Here you go. Let me know if you think this suspect fits the killer mold."

ANGEL FORCE WITNESS STATEMENT

Case File: #83-1104
Subject: Bartholomew Winters
Interviewer: Angel Marlow
Location: Badger's Haze Pawnbrokers, 42 Mist Street

ANGEL MARLOW: Please state your full name and occupation for the record.
WINTERS: Bartholomew Winters. I own the pawnshop. I've been here for twenty years.
ANGEL MARLOW: And your relationship to the deceased, Eliza Thorny?
WINTERS: We weren't friends, if that's what you're asking.
ANGEL MARLOW: Several witnesses

reported seeing you arguing with Miss Thorny in the square yesterday afternoon. Tell me what that was about.

WINTERS: It was a professional disagreement.

ANGEL MARLOW: Given the seriousness of this matter, I'll need more details.

WINTERS: She encroached on my territory. I work with water. Eliza worked with fire. But lately, she'd been experimenting with water magic. Taking my clients. Undercutting my prices. It's bad for business. And this store don't pay for itself, so I need the extra income.

ANGEL MARLOW: What work do they ask you to do?

WINTERS: People come to me when they need lost things found. I divine what's missing. And I'm damn good at it. I need that work, or my business will go under.

ANGEL MARLOW: You were angry with Eliza for taking your customers?

WINTERS: I was protecting my interests. For twenty years, I've been the only water practitioner in this place. Then she has the cheek to dabble in my element. That's called greed. And it was rude. Eliza didn't even ask. Our argument was about boundaries. We needed to set them back to how they were. Change is always bad. I can't think of a single person who likes change. It's uncomfortable.

ANGEL MARLOW: Did things get physical?

WINTERS: No! I don't hit women.

ANGEL MARLOW: But you have a temper?

WINTERS: I didn't say that. Everyone can get het up when something they care about is under threat.

ANGEL MARLOW: Did you threaten Miss Thorny?

WINTERS: I told her to stick to fire before she got burned. But it was a figure of speech. We all say dumb stuff when we're angry. I meant nothing by it. It wasn't a declaration that I planned on killing her. That would have been dumb. I'm not the brightest spark, but I know not to make stupid moves.

ANGEL MARLOW: Where were you between 10 PM last night and 6 AM this morning?

WINTERS: Home. Alone. I live above this store. I'm either in this store or at home.

ANGEL MARLOW: Can anyone verify that?

WINTERS: I don't keep company. I don't enjoy company. People annoy me. They're always saying or doing senseless twaddle.

ANGEL MARLOW: You have no alibi for the time of Miss Thorny's death?

WINTERS: I don't need one. I didn't kill her.

ANGEL MARLOW: Are you aware of any enemies Miss Thorny had?

WINTERS: Half the village. She wasn't liked. Talented, but arrogant. She thought she could master every element, but nature don't work that way. She should have stuck to what she knew. Then she wouldn't be dead.

ANGEL MARLOW: Is there anyone in particular who didn't like her or whom she had concerns about?

WINTERS: I already said, half the village.

ANGEL MARLOW: I need names.

WINTERS: Try Englebert Turgleton. She humiliated him recently. Did you know she turned down his proposal in front of the entire council when the idiot brought up an *any other business* item? Arrogant twonk got down on one knee and pulled out a ring. A man like that don't take rejection well.

ANGEL MARLOW: It was a marriage proposal?

WINTERS: He wasn't on one knee to tie his shoelace. The smug-faced toad was a joke. He was so angry when Eliza said no. It even made me smile to see him get what for. He almost popped a vein in his head and then tried to make a big joke about it, but we all knew he was serious. A serious knucklehead, thinking he could snag himself a looker like Eliza. And she was three times more powerful than him. The Thorny witches have serious magic in their blood. Or at least, they did. I don't think there are any left. Eliza's sister isn't spoken about, and the parents are dead.

ANGEL MARLOW: Our records show you owed Miss Thorny money.

WINTERS: Nope.

ANGEL MARLOW: Are you sure? Are our records wrong?

WINTERS: It was nothing.

ANGEL MARLOW: That depends on the sum owed.

WINTERS: Nothing big. I'd almost forgotten about it.

ANGEL MARLOW: If you could dredge your memory.

WINTERS: Fine. Fine. Three years ago, I needed more inventory for the store. I wanted to branch out and offer regular goods, not just items people pawn. Eliza had the cash, and we came to an arrangement. I was paying her back monthly, just as we agreed. It was all aboveboard.

ANGEL MARLOW: An arrangement that her death nullified?

WINTERS: You're reaching if you

think I'd kill Eliza over that. The loan was almost paid off. I have the receipts. You're looking in the wrong place. Go hassle the jilted jerk who has egg on his face.

ANGEL MARLOW: What can you tell me about Miss Thorny's recent experiments with water? What did she hope to achieve by adding a second element to her repertoire?

WINTERS: No clue. We weren't best buddies. All I can say is it was dangerous. She was combining opposing elements. It's not done. Elements fight each other. It's like putting two magnets together. You get pushback. The magical backlash would be a hot mess. And like I said, we all have our talents. Stick with those, and everything works out. Overstep, and this is what magic does to you.

ANGEL MARLOW: Is that what you think happened at the well?

WINTERS: Eliza bit off more than she could chew. That well has power. Old power. It's not to be messed with. And you add elemental powers that don't like each other, and boom. Something bad had to happen. Eliza was warned. I even warned her. So did her apprentice. Eliza never listened. The Thorny witches have always had enormous egos. I remember the mother. She was something else, but arrogant. That's just ugly.

ANGEL MARLOW: For someone who wasn't close to Miss Thorny, you know a lot about her affairs.

WINTERS: I work with water. The well is my business. My family has always watched the well. Every potent source of magic needs a guardian.

ANGEL MARLOW: Have you ever conducted experiments at the well?

WINTERS: Like what?

ANGEL MARLOW: To test the stability of the magic. As you said, it's old magic, and old magic distorts. It needs looking after.

WINTERS: By me and my ancestors. We ensure the magic stays calm. Samuel Greene cares for the rest. He's the well's caretaker. Nice guy. Doesn't say much, but you can rely on him.

ANGEL MARLOW: You were never curious about how far the magic could be pushed? Or what it could do for you?

WINTERS: I'm not suicidal. I know to respect magic. And I'm always careful about when I check the magic. Go there on a full moon, like Eliza, and you have to expect trouble.

ANGEL MARLOW: You knew she was planning something last night?

WINTERS: I... I saw Eliza buying supplies. Chalk. Candles. I asked her what she was doing, and she told me to mind my business. The well is my business.

ANGEL MARLOW: Did you follow Miss Thorny to see if she'd succeed with her plan to cast a spell around the well?

WINTERS: No. I told you. I was home. Right above your head.

ANGEL MARLOW: We found a blue thread caught on the well's edge. The color could match the sweater you're wearing. Do you have any objection if I take it to match the fabric?

WINTERS: It won't make a difference to my innocence or guilt. I was at the well yesterday, checking the water levels and making sure the magic was steady. Well, as steady as it'll ever be. It's my routine. The thread must have gotten caught then.

ANGEL MARLOW: How steady was the well magic?

WINTERS: It's seen better days. It dredges up old whispers from the past and plants them in ears if you're not paying attention. I know a few who've been driven mad by the twisted magic swirling in that water. Only an innocent or an idiot would wander around it without the proper wards. It's not been stable for some time. I told Eliza that too. I got ignored. What a surprise.

ANGEL MARLOW: Thank you for your time. We'll be in touch if we have more questions. Don't leave Badger's Haze.

WINTERS: I never do. I'm always here. I couldn't leave even if I wanted to. Someone has to monitor that well, or it'll destroy us all.

FINAL NOTES: The subject was initially hostile, but eventually cooperative. His alibi can't be verified. His knowledge of the victim's activities suggests a closer relationship than he admitted.

The clothing thread evidence is inconclusive. It could be from the earlier visit, as claimed. Mr. Winters is well known in Badger's Haze for his work protecting the well.

MOTIVE: Professional rivalry? The financial motive seems weak since a record check showed he owed less than five hundred when Miss Thorny died, and he was making regular monthly repayments. None were missed.

Chapter 6

I leaned in as the snow glove flared to life. "Did you get all of that? That was a long interview. Angel Force knew what they were doing back then. Shame they don't now or I wouldn't be stuck here."

Sage's face swam into focus. "I got it. Did Bartholomew do it? He's a water witch with a natural tie to the well. My book says the Winter family has been guarding that ancient power since the first records were kept. Maybe longer."

"He hated Eliza mixing elements. As guardian, he'd see it as his job to stop her." I sat back. "I need to see this well up close and personal."

Sage groaned. "Can't I get you to change your mind? You've barely got any magic to protect yourself. And you've got other suspects to check."

"I'll be careful."

"You're never careful, and you need to be. You're not all-powerful anymore."

"I don't need magic for everything," I said. "I'll only peek. But before I go to the scene of the crime, I need to question Bartholomew. And I've got a cunning plan."

Sage's whiskers twitched. "Cunning or dumb?"

"Rude. I'm the smartest cat in the village."

"With the least magic," Sage muttered.

"Meow! Cranky much? Did you sleep on your arthritic side again?"

"When you're my age, every side is the arthritic side."

"You just say that so Vorana carries you everywhere."

Sage sighed. "You got me. Tell me the genius plan."

"Only if you stop being defeatist."

"No promises."

"Fine. I'm scaring Bartholomew into talking. Maybe even confessing to murder."

"How? You've barely mastered kitten spells."

"Bartholomew is into old magic. And I've heard tales about a terrifying cat spirit who lives in Badger's Haze by the name of Whiskerbone. What if Whiskerbone visited him?"

"You can't summon Whiskerbone! I've heard of Whiskerbone. If you brought him to your paw with a summons, he'd eat you."

"I'm not summoning anything. I'm becoming Whiskerbone. With your help."

Sage's eyes narrowed. "Go on."

"I need a spell. Something simple. I'm working with rat droppings, moldy books, and a dying sense of dignity, so nothing obscure in the ingredients."

"That could work," Sage said slowly. "And I know just the spell to transform you. You'll need one drop of your blood, ghost thistle from the cemetery, green graveyard moss, not the lacy kind, and two foxglove petals."

"I can get all of that," I said. "Once it's mixed, what incantation do I need?"

Sage vanished from sight, and a book thudded down. "Here we are. Mix with rainwater and say: *From claw to purr, from breath to bone, let shadow stretch what light has known. I walk between. I speak untrue, and wear the fear that once I knew.*"

"Is this a glamor spell or an illusion?" I asked.

"Illusion. Your voice will sound wrong, your shadow will misbehave, and you'll smell nasty. It only lasts seven minutes, though. Burn the moss as a scent charm, and it'll follow you like the breath of the dead."

"Perfect. I know where Bartholomew lives. I'll trap him, scare him senseless, and he'll spill everything."

Sage chuckled. "Remember, seven minutes before the glamor fades. Use them well. The clock will be ticking."

With no time to waste, I slipped out of the library, the heavy oak door sighing shut behind me. The street beyond was half-swallowed by mist, nosing into every crack and shadow. Moonlight smeared pale streaks across the road.

First stop was the abandoned cemetery. It crouched on the edge of the village, its crooked gate dangling from one hinge. The hinges were engraved with protective glyphs, but they were so worn you couldn't tell if they were meant to keep things out or keep them in. Either way, they failed.

A larger, newer cemetery had replaced this one, and although I'd peered through the gate a few times, I did my best to respect graveyards and the fearsome guardians who protected them.

Inside this abandoned place, the air was thicker, like the ground exhaled slow, cold breaths. I walked between leaning gravestones carved with names no one had spoken in a century, searching for ghost thistle. It grew in tufts along the older plots, its pale stalks tipped with blossoms that glowed faintly in the gloom. I brushed against one and felt it shiver. The petals left a tingle on my paw when I plucked them, the magic faint but unmistakable.

Next came the graveyard moss. The green fuzzy kind. I found it clinging stubbornly to the base of a crumbling angel statue, whose face had worn away to a blank oval. The moss came up in a soft, damp clump, smelling faintly of rain and something sour.

Foxglove was trickier to find. I slipped back through the streets and discovered an overgrown garden behind an abandoned apothecary. The place was all brambles and shadows, but the foxglove grew tall and defiant. I plucked two petals, careful not to brush too close. Foxglove magic was a quiet, patient killer.

Rainwater was easy. Badger's Haze had puddles like other places had streetlamps. I found one in the dip of an uneven cobblestone, its surface reflecting a warped version of my perfect, fluffy white face. I dipped a small vial in, corked it, and slipped it into the satchel I'd liberated from the library's lost property box.

Last came the drop of blood. I'd save that for the moment of the spell, because I liked keeping my blood inside me until absolutely necessary.

I headed for the pawnshop. Shuttered shops lined the crooked street, their windows dark, their signs swaying. A string of wilted charms dangled from a doorway, the protective beads cracked and cloudy. The wards here didn't just fade, they seemed to get bored and give up.

Badger's Haze was quiet. Not peaceful quiet, but the kind that presses against your ears, making you think you'd lost your hearing just before something jumps out and chews your tail off.

Somewhere behind me, a door creaked open, then slammed shut. I didn't look back. That's how you got hexed in this place.

The pawnshop squatted at the end of Mist Street, hunched between two leaning buildings like it hid from the wind. Its sign hung askew, the painted letters flaking, and the faint scent of damp leather and candle smoke seeped from the cracks around the door.

Seven minutes of borrowed magic lay ahead of me. Seven minutes to make Bartholomew Winters spill what he knew.

A window had been left open an inch, so after checking no one watched me, I forced it wider, pausing to listen for movement inside, before dropping to the floor.

I followed Sage's instructions to the letter. Well, almost. I cut my paw too deep, so added too much blood to the spell, then muttered the rhyme over the mixture of rainwater and ingredients.

My voice warped on the last line of the spell, like I was speaking through a tin can filled with ash.

My paws shimmered around the edges, and I felt wrong. Not monstrous, exactly. Just subtly off.

I crept out with the moss smoldering in my paw, just as Sage had told me to do, and made my way up the stairs.

The illusion worked, but only just. My glorious white tail kept flickering in and out like bad television reception.

I climbed the stairs fast. Floorboards creaked beneath my paws, and the magic tightened, like it was crawling back onto the page and didn't want to help me.

I slipped through an unlocked door to Bartholomew's apartment and crept inside. He was hunched over a notebook, teacup forgotten, muttering something about root balance and offerings.

"Bartholomeeeew," I said, my voice a twisted echo of death and sass.

He jumped like a scalded toad, knocking over his chair.

"You broke your promise," I growled.

He scrambled back, eyes wide, fumbling for a silver herb scoop like it could protect him. "Who's there?"

"A reckoning with your past." I stepped into the dim light. My ghost-form rippled just enough to unsettle the soul. My eyes glowed. My claws scraped on the hardwood like the ticking of a clock counting down. "Eliza Thorny sends her regards."

"Whiskerbone? No, it can't be you," he choked. "You can't be here for me."

"Eliza is stuck. She sent me. She blames you for everything."

"Me! For what? I didn't do anything."

"She speaks your name in anger. You did a terrible thing to her. She sent me to punish you."

His eyes bulged as he pushed himself away from the table to escape me, as I huffed my deathly breath at him. "Stop. She asked for it!"

"What did she ask for? Her death?"

"Not death! Magic. She asked for magic."

"You gave her a spell?" I hissed. "You sent her to the well and then to her death with a tainted spell?"

"I... no, nothing like that." Bartholomew tilted his head, his eyes narrowing.

"What secret do you hide?" I hissed menacingly. "Answer me."

He gulped. "Eliza demanded a portal spell. I didn't know what she'd do with it. I never thought she'd use it at the well. No one would be that crazy."

"You know the well takes. Your family has kept it calm for thousands of years, yet you gave Eliza portal magic when you knew her interest in the well. What did you think she'd do with it?"

"I didn't ask. She said if I got her a portal spell to connect to the well water, my debt would be repaid."

"You wanted Eliza gone. She interfered with something you believed was yours."

His face twisted, panic and horror crawling across his skin as I lifted a paw in a threat move. "Eliza was obsessed! She said the well whispered to her in dreams. I told her not to go near it, but she never listened."

Four minutes left. My voice cracked, and the illusion shimmered. My white tail flickered into view. Panic bubbled. I had to push for more information before it was too late.

"Eliza trusted you," I snarled. "You unlocked a dangerous door and let her walk through it! Confess what you did. You led her to her doom."

Bartholomew collapsed to his knees. "The well must have wanted her. It always wants someone. I just...I just thought it would stop once it had her. I thought giving the spell to Eliza would end its instability. I tried everything to calm it, but nothing worked. It wasn't due another sacrifice, but something must have gone wrong. I don't know. The magic is complex."

"You offered Eliza to the well, so you as good as killed her." I stalked forward until I was nose to nose with him.

"I'm not the strongest witch in my family, but I do my best. And everything was fine until Eliza got involved and started casting spells. She was always pushing. It made me angry. She had no right. The Thorny witches had so much already, but she wanted more."

Two minutes left. My fur rippled. My back paw turned solid again. The spell was dying.

"I gave her the magic. It was up to her what she did with it." He looked up, eyes wide, and confusion crossed his face. "Wait! You're not—"

I let out a guttural growl and hissed before turning and running down the stairs. The window I'd come through had swung closed, but I spotted an open floor vent. It was small and would be filthy, but I should fit through.

I dove. Headfirst. I jammed my shoulder and bent my ear backward. Thick black dust coated my fur. Something wet squelched beneath my back paw. I didn't want to know what it was. I squeezed through with a screech that was decidedly not ghostly.

The spell collapsed in a puff of moss-scented air just as I tumbled out of the store into an alley and back into my regular, exhausted, fur-matted, panting self.

I lay there for a moment, catching my breath. Then I limped home. Dignity? Gone. Fur? Ruined.

But I had information.

Bartholomew gave Eliza a dangerous portal spell. He encouraged her to use the well, despite knowing how unstable it was.

Did the well want Eliza? Or did Bartholomew guide her to it because he was terrified he'd lost control and would be shamed for failing in his duties?

Operation Whiskerbone was a success.

But goddesses, did I need an enormous plate of salmon after that stinky mission.

Chapter 7

Bright and early the next morning, the snow globe flickered, light spilling across the library table in fractured shards. Sage's face swam into view, a little distorted, like she was trapped in a bubble at the bottom of the sea.

"Hey!" she called, her voice muffled. "Is that soot in your fur, or is this thing on the blink again?"

"Greetings! And it's worse than soot. I had to squish through a floor vent to escape Bartholomew. Grubby, dusty, full of mouse bones," I said. "My tail will never fluff right again with the amount of gross, unidentifiable goo attached to it."

"You need a hot soak and three hours of grooming."

"I have been grooming for three hours! I need a new life. Preferably one where I'm not crawling through vents pretending to be a ghost to scare confessions out of morally questionable pawnbrokers with more secrets than sense."

Her grin sharpened. "It worked, though?"

"Oh, it worked. Bartholomew believed I was Whiskerbone, come to hex his soul because of Eliza."

Sage leaned closer to the globe. "What did he say?"

"He helped Eliza tap into the well's power. He gave her a portal spell, even though he knew how dangerous it was. I think he lied about the risk because he wanted her dead."

Sage's ears flicked back. "You're saying Bartholomew offered Eliza to the well?"

"Not exactly. He didn't lead her there, but he gave her something to unlock trouble she couldn't handle. In his statement, he ranted about her ego. He must have wanted to squash it and hoped the well would do it for him."

Sage's whiskers drooped. "That well sounds cursed. Or worse. Alive and hungry. Maybe it is our killer. How do you lock up an all-powerful, unstable well?"

"You don't. And the well didn't do it. A magical hand was involved." My booping snooter twitched. "Hey! Are you eating a sausage?"

"No," Sage said far too quickly, "but I've got half a smoked herring and a saucer of cream. It's part of my second breakfast. Want me to slide it through the globe?"

"I hate you," I muttered. "All I've had is some out-of-date jerky from the abandoned store on the corner. It barely filled a gap. My belly pooch is a distant memory."

She patted her middle smugly. "Mine's growing. So, what's your next move?"

"Magic needs direction," I said. "Bartholomew knew what he gave Eliza was dangerous and hoped she'd mess up, but is he our killer? I'm not convinced."

"You should confront him again. Maybe your version of Whiskerbone wasn't scary enough to get him to confess."

I shook my head. "The illusion faded too soon, so I can't go back as Whiskerbone. He'd know I was an impostor. That won't work again."

Sage thumped a paw on the snow globe. "You're saying my spell was a dud?"

"I may have added too much blood," I admitted. "But my suggestion that he was a killer genuinely shocked him. That wasn't an act. We should check the other suspects, see if someone else stands out."

"Who do you want to tackle next?" she asked.

"Vera Blackling. She was Eliza's apprentice for years. Perhaps she saw something she shouldn't."

"She must have known Eliza experimented with the well's magic. Maybe she wanted a piece of it, but Eliza refused to share."

"Or Vera wanted out, and Eliza wouldn't let her go." I reached for the folder at my side. "I'll send through her statement. You can read it while you stuff your face and listen to my stomach gripe with hunger."

"You could always catch a mouse."

I snorted. "Not in Badger's Haze. The mice here are the size of small terriers, carry switchblades, and fling magic like it's confetti at an ogre wedding. I'm not risking my whiskers for a mouthful of trouble."

Her laughter bubbled through the snow globe, warm and sharp. "Send me that statement. I want to see what Vera's hiding."

"On its way." I slid the file toward the globe. "And when you're done reading, I might pay Vera a little visit."

WITNESS STATEMENT
CASE FILE: #83-1104
SUBJECT: BLACKLING, VERA
INTERVIEWER: ANGEL ABEL
LOCATION: ANGEL FORCE REGIONAL OFFICE.

ANGEL ABEL: Please state your full name and occupation for the record.
BLACKLING: Vera Blackling. I was Eliza Thorny's apprentice.
ANGEL ABEL: Was that a full-time position?
BLACKLING: Yes. I'm also studying for my magical certification. I was supposed to take the exam soon. I want to teach.
ANGEL ABEL: Supposed to? What happened?
BLACKLING: Life. You know. It's always complicated. Eliza kept me busy. So busy that I don't know what to do now she's gone. I still can't believe this has happened.
ANGEL ABEL: I'm sorry for your loss. How would you describe your

relationship with Miss Thorny?

BLACKLING: She was my mentor.

ANGEL ABEL: And was that satisfactory? You enjoyed being mentored by her?

BLACKLING: Yes! I mean, Eliza was talented. Powerful. The Thorny witches are legendary. I learned a lot.

ANGEL ABEL: But?

BLACKLING: But sometimes Eliza kept things from me. Secrets.

ANGEL ABEL: Secrets concerning what?

BLACKLING: Her experiments with magic.

ANGEL ABEL: Did this cause friction between you?

BLACKLING: No. Eliza was a private person and tried things most of us would never dare to do. Maybe she bent magical rules, but she kept it to herself so she wouldn't get in trouble. She was protecting me.

ANGEL ABEL: Witnesses place you arguing with Miss Thorny the evening before her death. What did you argue about?

BLACKLING: Nothing important. We disagreed about a magical technique. I thought Eliza was being reckless. I shouldn't have said anything. It wasn't my place. I was the student and there to learn.

ANGEL ABEL: Reckless how?

BLACKLING: Eliza was trying things she shouldn't have.

ANGEL ABEL: Specifically?

BLACKLING: I... I don't want to say. Even though she's dead, I don't want her reputation messed with. Eliza was a good witch.

ANGEL ABEL: This is a murder investigation, Miss Blackling. Any information could help us discover how Miss Thorny died.

BLACKLING: Eliza worked with the well, trying to combine fire and water magic. It was dangerous. Even I knew that. You work with a single element. You have to master that. It can take a lifetime.

ANGEL ABEL: Dangerous enough to kill her?

BLACKLING: Maybe. Some people say the well magic can't be trusted. Eliza laughed at that idea. She tried to amplify the magic, but it's too unpredictable. Especially when using opposing elements.

ANGEL ABEL: Unpredictable how?

BLACKLING: The well has ancient power. Did you know Eliza wasn't the first to die by the well? There have to be offerings. Magic users who give themselves willingly. But she wouldn't listen to any warnings. Eliza tried to control it. To bind the magic to her will. Magic that old will never be tamed. It shouldn't be.

ANGEL ABEL: Is that what you argued about?

BLACKLING: It wasn't an argument as such. A professional disagreement. It was nothing.

ANGEL ABEL: Witnesses heard you say: 'Eliza. You'll destroy us all.' Were you scared you'd be harmed?

BLACKLING: Not by Eliza, but I was worried things were out of control. Eliza was pushing too hard.

ANGEL ABEL: Were you scared enough to threaten Eliza about what would happen if she didn't stop?

BLACKLING: I didn't threaten her! I was warning her. I cared about her. I wish she hadn't been so arrogant, but she thought she was the only one who understood the well. There are families in Badger's Haze who have cared for the well for years.

ANGEL ABEL: Who else thinks they understand how the well works?

BLACKLING: Anyone who's lived here long enough. I'm not naming names. I don't want to get anyone in trouble.

ANGEL ABEL: Miss Blackling, you don't want me to think you're obstructing a murder investigation, do you?

BLACKLING: I'm not! I'm just scared.

ANGEL ABEL: Scared of what?

BLACKLING: The well. What if Eliza was murdered to hide a truth about it? Something she uncovered when testing her powers.

ANGEL ABEL: What truth?

BLACKLING: Eliza said she'd harnessed the well's power to open portals. But that was impossible.

ANGEL ABEL: Do you know anyone who might have wanted to harm Miss Thorny because of her knowledge about the well?

BLACKLING: That's an easy one. Bartholomew Winters. He hated her testing the well. He didn't think she understood what she was doing. Oh! And Englebert. He was angry when she turned down his proposal. We had a giggle about that, but maybe we shouldn't. He was so unhappy.

ANGEL ABEL: Since we're establishing timelines to get a full picture of Eliza's last movements, please tell me where you were between 10 PM on November 14th and 6 AM on November 15th.

BLACKLING: At home. In my apartment. I was studying, then I went to sleep.

ANGEL ABEL: Can anyone verify this?

BLACKLING: No. I live alone. It's only a studio, so no room for guests or roommates. It does me, but it's cramped. Cheap, though. Apprentices don't get paid much. That's why I plan on teaching.

ANGEL ABEL: So, you have no alibi for the time of Eliza's death?

BLACKLING: I don't need one. Eliza helped me improve my magic. I wanted to be like her. Well, not pushing so many boundaries, but I wanted to be strong and sure of my magic. I'd never hurt Eliza. I lost a friend and a mentor when she died. I don't know what I'll do without her. Maybe I should find a new mentor. There aren't any in Badger's Haze, so I'll have to move. I don't want to move. I like it here.

ANGEL ABEL: Is there anything else you can think of that's relevant to our investigation?

BLACKLING: Did you find Eliza's diary? It was more like a personal journal and grimoire combined. I never got a look inside, but there could be something in there to help.

ANGEL ABEL: Thank you, Miss Blackling. I'll make a note.

BLACKLING: Does that mean you didn't find it? When you do, I'd like to keep it. It'll help with my studies.

ANGEL ABEL: No journal has shown

up, but we'll log it as evidence if it does. For now, don't leave Badger's Haze. We may have more questions.

CONCLUDING NOTE: The subject appeared nervous. Her lack of an alibi and knowledge of the victim's activities is suspicious. Her description of the argument with the victim doesn't match the witness reports, which showed their argument was intense.

RECOMMENDATIONS: Review the evidence log for a personal grimoire journal. If not found, send an officer to check Eliza's home and store.

Chapter 8

I lounged on the desk in the library, the snow globe warm beneath my paw. "What did you think about Vera's interview?"

Sage's whiskers quivered inside the glass. "She sounded guilty about something. And apprentices snoop. I bet she prowled through Eliza's things when she wasn't around and found something she shouldn't have. And that alibi? Weak. Limp as overcooked noodles."

"She seemed nervous," I said. "But was it because she was hiding something or because she was scared?"

"Scared of the well?"

"Maybe. Or scared of being caught in a lie." I flicked my tail toward the far shelves, where ghost-light seeped from between the books. "Vera knows more than she admitted when the angels questioned her."

Sage leaned closer to the glass. "What about those secrets Eliza kept in her grimoire? What's in there?"

"That's what I want to find out. She'd have recorded everything when researching the well magic and how to access a portal. We need that grimoire journal."

"It never showed up in the evidence log?" Sage asked.

"Not a trace. The angels must have missed it, or someone stole it."

"Eliza didn't sound trusting. She'd have hidden it somewhere tricky to find. Angel Force probably didn't look hard enough."

"It has to be somewhere no one would ever think to look."

"Her store?" Sage suggested. "Her home? It's been years since she died, so someone's probably cleared everything out by now. They'd have dumped the journal in error."

"If the angels fumbled the search, that grimoire could still be tucked away. It might answer all our questions."

"Or cause a dozen new ones," Sage said. "Are you going to look for it?"

"What else can I do? Sprawl here, eating salmon? That grimoire is the key to understanding what happened to Eliza all those years ago."

"You're too optimistic."

"And you're too pessimistic," I shot back. "We'll see who's right."

❧❧❧❧ ❧❧❧❧

I waited until dark to visit Eliza's cottage. According to what I'd pieced together from the case file, her personal grimoire never surfaced. It had remained hidden all these years, and inside those pages would be records of her experiments, tensions in the village, and maybe even who her latest crush was. Wasn't that what everyone wrote about in their secret diary, no matter their age?

The wind changed as I walked up the overgrown path toward Eliza's front door, less like a breeze and more like a hot, wet breath, straight from the lungs of something that shouldn't be breathing. I hoped that wasn't a prelude to what I'd find inside.

The garden was a wild tangle, proving no one had touched the place since Eliza died. Maybe the villagers thought she haunted the building, or the place was cursed because of what happened to her.

There was a creepy, sagging scarecrow in the front yard. I hissed at it to show it I wasn't to be messed with. The thing had no idea my magic was on an extended vacation and left me as feeble as a newborn kitten.

The front door was swollen and warped, and no matter how hard I shoved, it wouldn't budge, so I squeezed through a gap in the frame. The air inside the cottage was damp. Mildew, old magic, and just a hint of honeysuckle and chalk dust tickled my booping snooter. Dust lay thick as wool, and spiderwebs draped across the furniture like sticky shrouds.

"Eliza? Are you still here?" I whispered, not expecting an answer, but it was comforting to make a noise in such a silent, forgotten tomb.

I started in a small, messy study, where Eliza had kept her books and magical brews, all dried out from neglect. The desk was overturned, drawers scattered, and one corner was scorched as if someone had flung a small fireball at it.

I pawed at a warped floorboard and discovered a gap beneath. There was nothing in there. Perhaps whoever made such a mess of this place had found whatever was in that space. It had better not be the grimoire.

The kitchen was worse, with the contents of drawers scattered on the floor. But the genuine horror was in the bedroom. The room looked untouched at first. The bed was made if dusty, and candles had melted into smooth stubs. There was a photo on the nightstand. Eliza and someone I didn't recognize. Whoever he was, he was handsome.

I was about to jump on the bed for a better look when the rug moved. I've seen some out of this world grab you by the throat and make you squeak things in my nine lives. Hexed hedgehogs, possessed voodoo dolls, a banshee with murderous intent, and an evil goblin, but that rug shifting like a slumbering beast? That was new.

I backed away slowly, tail fluffed to maximum volume and hackles lifted for full menacing effect.

"Not today. I'm on a mission for justice." I pulled myself to my full height. "House, I'm here to help Eliza. I know she was murdered, and I must learn why. Who killed her? Where did she hide her secrets? You can offer ideas if you like, but don't be foolish and get in my way. These murder mittens don't play nicely."

The air stilled. Was the house listening, or was it about to unleash a fresh horror on me?

A plank loosened close to the bed and fell, revealing a hidden nook. There was no journal inside, but there was a pouch of dried herbs, a cracked crystal, and a note written in smudged pencil: *The truth is below. Don't trust the light. Ask the moths.*

Cryptic? Absolutely. But helpful? Possibly.

I left the room before the rug lunged at me and rolled me up inside it, taking the note and bolting to the living room. The fireplace flared out bursts of blue, green, then red flames, licking toward me with malice. Something spelled out in soot on the wall *go home*.

I hissed. I would if I could.

That was when the note I'd tucked in my mouth seared against my whiskers. I yelped, dropped it, and read it again, hissing the words under my breath as I wriggled my singed whiskers.

The truth is below. Don't trust the light. Ask the moths.

Below. That must mean the cellar.

I turned in a slow circle, ears alert, booping snooter twitching, and hunted for several minutes before finding the entrance to a cellar through the trapdoor in the kitchen pantry.

It was the last place I wanted to go. Going down there was like asking to be hexed in five creative ways, and I had next to no magic to protect myself. In horror movies, you should never go into the cellar, but someone always did, and what happened to them? We all know it never ended well.

Still, my curiosity had always been stronger than fear. And I had a murder to solve. Doing so would get me a paw step closer to Zandra. And I'd do anything to return home.

I tugged on the small cord handle, and the door whipped up as if the hinges had been oiled. A bright, welcoming light greeted me, and I smelled freshly baked bread and a yummy fish dish. I took a step and stopped.

Don't trust the light.

But that smell was so good. I missed fresh fish so badly my stomach ached with longing.

No! I must resist. The note was helping me find the personal grimoire. I turned away from temptation and returned to the living room.

My tail twitched as I scanned the room again. It was stuffed with the debris of Eliza's life. There were potion vials on side tables, a chessboard mid-game with cobwebs slung between bishop and knight, a shawl draped over an armchair like she might come back and curl up there at any moment.

But then, there, above the mantel. I hadn't noticed it before. A line of carved moths, no bigger than paw-sized, etched in dark wood along the upper molding. Eight of them. Each slightly different. One had wings outspread. One with antennae curled back. One perched as if mid-flight.

Ask the moths.

I hopped onto the mantle and inspected the carvings. One moth had a slight indentation behind the wing. Just enough space for a claw.

Curious, I pressed it.

Click.

The wall behind the fireplace gave a faint groan, like something old and sleepy stirred.

I pressed the moth with downward-angled wings. Click.

Another sound. Deeper this time. Beneath the floorboards. It felt like the house was opening some old secret to me. Or rather, my new moth friends were. I'd never chase another moth again if this worked.

One by one, I tested the carvings. Press. Listen. Wait. The fifth and seventh triggered something, too. And when I pressed the final one, the smallest, barely a nub of wood shaped like a folded-winged moth, a whir of ancient magic whispered through the room like a breeze from the other side.

The carved moths peeled off the wall. Not wood anymore. Their edges shimmered, cracked, and unfolded, shedding bark like old skin. One by one, they came alive, their wooden wings transforming into soft velvet. They fluttered from the trim with an eerie grace, glowing faintly.

They flew to the far wall behind Eliza's velvet armchair. The moths hovered there, tracing the outline of a nearly invisible crack.

So that's what the note meant! The moths didn't just know. They *revealed.*

I hopped down and walked across the floor. One moth landed delicately on my booping snooter as I approached, then veered off toward the base of the wall as if encouraging me to investigate.

I raised a paw and swatted gently at the hairline fracture. The plaster crumbled like ash, as if it had been waiting for a sign before revealing whatever was hidden behind it. A few more swipes and the wall gave way with a dry sigh, revealing a narrow stone passage.

The moths took flight, swirling around me in an eclipse of color and wind. If I wasn't so intent on solving this puzzle, my murder mittens would have gotten to work. But no. You didn't murder your friends, no matter how tempting their wings looked.

Instead, I whispered a thank you to my winged companions and cautiously stepped into the passage, where I could just see a set of steps. The air changed immediately. Damp and cold.

I looked back once. The fire in the hearth flared violently. A glowing script blinked once with the word 'go' before sputtering out entirely.

A tickle of surprise hit me as my moth companions guided me, lighting the way not with flame, but with a soft, silvery glow like moonlight on water. Other than the stuffy library ghosts, I'd been alone since my banishment to Badger's Haze, so I welcomed this company.

Down the stone steps I went, into the house's belly and into the secrets Eliza hid.

At the bottom, the air grew thick. My whiskers twitched as I smelled candle wax, rotted herbs, and something else. Something coppery. I knew that scent. Blood. I really hoped it wasn't blood. It was so hard to get out of white fur.

The chamber was square, carved into the rock beneath Eliza's home, the walls thick with lichen and etched with sigils that pulsed faintly under the moth-light. The center of the room held a stone pedestal waist-high to a human.

On top of it sat a box. Not ornate, just a small, hand-carved wooden box with a lock shaped like an eye.

Behind it, something glimmered.

Walking closer, I kept watch for anything lurking in the shadowy corners.

The back wall shimmered with magic, but it was an imperfect veil, suggesting the magic had degraded. It smelled of moonwort, a typical herb used as part of a concealment or visual spell.

A moth drifted toward it and passed through, flickering briefly, then vanished.

I didn't follow. That moth may not return. Instead, I looked at the box. And that was when I saw the journal! Not inside the box but wedged beneath the pedestal, protected from rot and time by a clever stasis charm. The spell was fading, though, and threads of it shimmered like dew.

I pulled it free, and it fell open on the last page. It was unfinished. Ink trailed off like Eliza had been pulled away mid-sentence. The final paragraph was little more than a scrawl.

The well spoke. Not in words, but in images. I saw my mother's hands in the water today. They were pulling me down. The light lies. The light shows only what the well wants you to believe. I've hidden the rest. If they find it, they will destroy the truth. They want to destroy everything. But I won't let them. I will...

The rest was smeared. Water damage? Maybe tears.

The moths swarmed around the magic on the back wall and pressed their wings to it in a perfect pattern. The spell shattered like glass, and what lay behind it wasn't another hidden room.

It was a memory. A preserved moment, looping in time. Eliza! She stood at the edge of the Badger's Haze well. Her hair was unbound, and her hands were shaking. And someone whose face I couldn't see stood behind her. Whispering.

No sound. Just the image of a blurred shadow. They held out a twisted, clawed hand, and light poured from it.

Eliza turned to look, and her eyes widened in horror. That was the moment. The moment she believed this person was helping. And that belief had killed her.

It wasn't the well that lured her to her death. It was the lie this mysterious individual had told her to get her to the well and cast that devastating magical blow.

The vision cracked and crumbled, vanishing into nothing as the moths retreated. One lingered and rested on my paw. Its wings glowed softly, then folded in.

I dragged the journal up the stairs and found a small satchel to shove it in. It was cumbersome on my back, but I didn't have far to go.

These were the times when I most missed Zandra. She was so good at carrying things, including me. I longed to rest on her shoulders while she walked, and I watched the world go by, content in my wonderful witch's safe embrace.

But I had the personal grimoire journal. And that would lead us to the truth and me back home.

The second I returned to the library, I tried to reach Sage, but the snow globe wasn't playing.

I thumped it. It glowed for a second but faded to black. When Sage reappeared, I'd tell her everything.

Chapter 9

The snow globe shimmered on the desk beside me, catching the pale morning light filtering through the cracked windows of the library. The faint scent of damp paper and ghost-lilies hung in the air as Sage's face flickered inside the globe.

We'd just spent twenty minutes catching up following my adventure at Eliza's cottage last night.

"Wait! Do you have scrambled eggs?" I flicked an ear.

"Maybe. I was trying to hide them from you." Sage nudged the plate out of view.

"I'm grateful this globe doesn't have a smell function."

She grinned. "I need brain food to digest everything you told me about Eliza's creepy old cottage. Are you still torturing yourself with that powdered oatmeal you found in the back of the cupboard?"

"It's a tradition now that I've eaten the last of the jerky." I curled my tail around my paws. "A terrible, soul-crushing tradition."

"You could conjure breakfast if your magic worked," Sage said with a shrug. "Or if you actually practiced the old ways."

I rolled my eyes toward the sagging shelves around me. "Thank you for reminding me about the giant magical void where my powers used to be. I hadn't noticed at all, what with sacrificing myself for the good of Crimson Cove. You know, your town."

Sage's gaze softened. "*Our* town. Sorry. That was mean. Your magic is amazing. Now that I've stopped setting fire to things, I'm enjoying using it. And honestly, I'm impressed you survived that visit to Eliza's house."

"An almost magical cat always succeeds when she makes a plan."

Sage laughed. "You always say that right before you nearly die."

"In truth, for a few minutes, I thought that was it when the rug shifted about like a wild beast emerging from hibernation. End of story."

"But you found the hidden grimoire." She leaned closer to the glass, a few flecks of egg stuck in her whiskers. "That's what matters."

I tapped a paw on the desk. "A sliver more sympathy wouldn't go amiss. Fighting with no magic is exhausting, and bruises take longer to heal. I'm making brave sacrifices for justice."

Sage gave me a look that said she wasn't fooled. "We both know why you're really doing this. So, what's in it? Confessions? Forbidden spells? A scandalous love affair?"

"I only glanced at the pages in the cottage," I admitted. "I figured we'd go through it together. Huh. That's strange."

"What?"

"I think I picked up the wrong journal." I nosed at the stack of books beside me, their spines cracked and titles long faded. "This place is such a mess. No one puts anything back where it belongs, and there is no fussy librarian to tidy the stacks or glare at noisy patrons. Where is it?"

"Did your ghost friends move the journal?"

"If it has been moved, it would have been the library rats," I said. "They could drag in a full-grown hellhound and make him sorry he was ever born."

"Shall I order more eggs while you figure things out?"

"Stop making me hungry, or I'll lose focus." I turned back to the journal I'd originally opened and drew in a sharp breath. "Oh! We have a problem."

"A ghostly problem or a giant killer rat problem?"

"An invisible problem."

"Ghosts can be invisible."

"No! It's not that. The journal pages are blank. Every page is empty. Last night it was full, humming with power. Now it's silent."

"Could the text be concealed?" Sage asked. "Eliza's magic was elemental. Try fire to reveal the words."

"I'm all out of matches."

"You still haven't mastered a basic fire spell?"

"No magic is basic when it's been ripped away," I said. "And fire spells are tricky. Eat your eggs. I'll work something out."

"Try water," Sage suggested.

"Maybe enchanted water from the well would work, but if I use water on the pages, I could destroy this journal, and then we'd be back to square one."

"Stay away from that well," Sage cautioned.

"It might be the only thing that triggers the journal." I sat back. "Fire was Eliza's natural element, but she worked hard to control water. She might have tied both elements to this journal to stop just anyone from reading the contents."

"The words vanished to protect her secrets." Sage's voice was distorted as she gorged on more eggs.

I ignored my grumbling stomach and her wanton show of gluttony. "Possibly. Or the journal needs a password."

"Blood magic could do it," Sage said. "A drop of Eliza's blood."

"Unfortunately, I'm fresh out of our victim's blood," I replied. "And there's no easy way to get any blood from a body buried for over twenty years."

Sage tilted her head. "What about moonlight? Or dragon breath?"

"No dragons around and it's daytime," I said, "but I have matches. A small, controlled flame could work."

"Or blow up in your face."

"It's an informed hunch. Detectives always follow their instincts."

"You're not a detective."

"I'm a super sleuth. That's much better." The hiss of a match flaring filled the air. I held the tiny flame close to the journal.

Sage grumbled most likely rude words under her breath. "What do you see?"

"Still blank. Wait... there's a shimmer. Oh, no!"

"What now?"

"The match dropped."

"Where?"

"On a pile of research notes."

"Juno!"

"It's fine. I'm stamping on it. Ow! Hot! Okay, now I'm fanning it. Oh, now the rug's caught. Well, it was ugly anyway. I'm dumping my watery oatmeal on it." A hiss of steam rose, filling the air with the smell of burned parchment and faintly sweet grains. "There. It's out. And now the library smells like cookies. Zandra would love it."

"Focus! Are you okay? Did the journal get damaged?"

"Singed whiskers, oatmeal on my tail, but alive."

"And the journal?"

"Untouched."

"Fire didn't work."

"The pages are still blank," I said.

"So now what?"

I stared hard at the empty pages. "The well water."

"That's too dangerous," Sage said. "I'll ask Vorana about spells that conceal words. Stay there. No dashing off to a haunted well. Promise me."

"I make no promises," I said.

"Juno!"

"Fine. No dying today in a weird, whispering, possibly hexed well."

"Good. Because if you disappear into its depths, I'm not coming after you."

"You can't. Angel Force ejects anyone who tries to enter Badger's Haze to get me out."

"I know. We've been trying," Sage said.

I hesitated. "Even Cythera?"

"Well, no, of course not. Finn had a go, though."

"He did?" I smiled. "I knew he'd be on my side."

"He got a reprimand and was docked a week's pay."

"Cythera is too tough. But if solving this case proves my worth, Angel Force has to let me come home."

"Only if you survive the well," Sage said.

"As if I'd let a power-hungry well harm me," I said. "Now, find me an answer to reveal these words, or it's time to go well hopping."

Chapter 10

My eyes ached from hours of poring over the library's ancient catalog, the pages smelling faintly of mildew and dried ink.

I leaned closer to the snow globe until my whiskers brushed the cool glass, waiting for Sage. "I'm cross-eyed from all the research, and I've hit a dead end. This catalog is so out of date. Tell me you found something amazing that will crack open the grimoire."

Sage's face appeared, her expression flat. "I've spent the day cross-referencing forbidden ink spells, charm-sealed texts, cursed calligraphy, and three theories that involved owl spit. Owl spit!"

"And?"

"Nothing solid," Sage said. "Vorana couldn't help, either. She came up with the same suggestions I'd found. You really couldn't find anything on your end?"

I slumped back against the chair, my tail curling tight around my paws. "I have all the magical strength of a damp biscuit right now. I tried to light a candle with a whisper charm and nearly set my whiskers on fire. It's gone, Sage. My magic has deserted me. I feel the need to mourn."

Her voice sharpened. "Then you shouldn't go near the well. Not without backup and someone with working magic."

"I was thinking about submerging the journal," I said, choosing to ignore the worry in Sage's voice. "Just enough to check for a concealment spell. Eliza died at the well, so her secrets wouldn't have wandered far."

"You want to dip a possibly immensely powerful and potentially cursed journal into a haunted well on your own?"

I lifted a shoulder in a slow shrug. "There's no proof of a curse. Or an evil well ghost. And we've found nothing in this library or Vorana's store to help. So yes, that's the plan. Tonight. The well water is perfect because it is magic. Old and strong."

"More like grumpy and unstable," Sage muttered. "If you get caught, you could end up stuffed and mounted on some weird witch's mantel."

"I'm doing it," I said. "I dunk the journal, we make progress, we solve this case, and I go free. Perfect solution."

"If something drags you in, you're on your own. I still don't like it."

"Neither do I," I admitted, "but the pages are hiding something. Eliza knew she was in trouble. This might tell us who killed her."

A faint sound pricked my ears. It was low and muffled. My head snapped toward the shadowed alcove where the library's scroll cases leaned in a dusty row.

"What was that?" Sage asked. "Did you whoop?"

"That wasn't my whoop," I said, my fur lifting along my spine. "Something just shifted over there."

"Don't joke, Juno."

"No joke." My voice dropped to a whisper. "I've felt watched all day. I thought it was the nosy library ghosts, but this feels different." My gaze locked onto the dark space between two sagging shelves. "Eyes! I just saw eyes. Two of them. Glowing."

"You need to go. Now. Sneak very fast."

"It's too late for that." The air tightened around me. My claws slid from their sheaths. "Whatever it is, it's looking right at me."

I risked a glance at the snow globe. The connection dropped. I was alone.

Chapter 11

The snow globe's glow faded, leaving the library bathed in a stale, dusty hush. I sat for a moment, my ears swiveling toward every creak and sigh of the old building. The scent of scorched oatmeal still lingered from earlier, but underneath it, something sharper had crept in.

It wasn't the usual musty paper smell or the faint perfume of ghost lilies. This was different. It had a damp dog tang. My whiskers quivered. Something was in here with me.

I slid off the desk and crept into an aisle, keeping my belly low to the floor. The wooden boards groaned in protest under my paws, and I paused between each step, listening.

A shadow moved at the edge of my vision, melting behind the stacks. My tail stiffened. I followed, weaving between leaning bookcases and ancient scroll racks. The smell grew stronger, laced with a faint trace of fur and something wild.

I got to a corner, where the light barely reached. That was when I heard it. A low, deliberate scrape, like claws testing the floorboards. Slow. Purposeful. Close.

I turned. Nothing. Then a low growl, right in my left ear.

The bookshelves blurred as I ducked into the aisle between *Hex Histories* and *Traditional Household Spells for the Modern Trad Wife*. A stack of dusty scrolls exploded behind me as my pursuer skidded around the corner. It was another cat. Gray, scruffy fur, and with murder in his eyes.

"You're sniffing where you shouldn't sniff!" he snarled.

I vaulted over a fallen pile of books.

The cat lunged, and I felt the brush of his teeth on my back leg. I slid under a reading table, kicked a chair behind me, and heard the glorious sound of him faceplanting into it, giving me two seconds of breathing room. I took them.

Then a hiss, and there he was again, his eyes blazing, fur sparking with magic.

"She was mine," he spat. "You're not worthy of her secrets. Stay out of our business."

"Who are we talking about?" I dodged a paw swipe and kept running.

"Eliza. She was my witch."

I scrambled up a book stack, kicking books onto his head. I glanced back at him. "I didn't know Eliza had a familiar."

"Leave this alone. Stop messing with her memories. She's suffered enough. You want to steal everything she held dear."

"I'm not trying to steal anything." I almost lost my footing and clung to a shelf, my back legs flailing. "I'm trying to find out who killed her!"

"You'll only make it worse. Go away!"

I twisted, narrowly dodged a chomp aimed at my neck, and landed in a pile of scrolls on a desk. The cat barreled past me, skidded, rebounded off a shelf labeled *Minor Curses*, and came right back.

He was not quitting.

I dove for the stairs, and he was right behind me. Claw swipes. Teeth snaps. This cat meant to kill me.

We hit the top landing. I did a spin that would have made a ballerina proud, bounced off the wall, and shot down the next corridor like an enchanted broomstick.

And then nothing. Silence. No claws. No breath. No biting. The cat was gone. Had I lost him?

I stopped. Waited. Looked behind me.

The corridor was empty.

Then, a whisper from the shadows. "You open that journal wrong, and Eliza won't forgive you. I was supposed to protect her. I failed, but I won't again. And she won't let me. She haunts my dreams, and she'll haunt your nightmares."

I didn't answer, just backed away slowly. My tail puffed, and my mouth dry.

"You need to leave," the cat snarled.

"I can't!"

"I'll make you."

"I have to stay in Badger's Haze. It's my punishment. While I'm here, I want to help those in trouble. What's your name?"

There was a long silence.

"I'm Roland." Eliza's broken, furious, sharp-toothed familiar slunk from the shadows. He looked like a cat who got caught in a downpour and hadn't dried out. His gray fur was puffed in weird directions, and he had half an ear missing. He smelled like a wet dishcloth.

"Well, Roland, familiar to the late Eliza Thorny, greetings! When you're quite done trying to kill me, we have a lot to talk about."

I paced in front of the snow globe, my tail flicking with leftover irritation from my latest library encounter.

"What happened? I lost the connection at a crucial moment." Sage's voice drifted through the glassy shimmer. "Are you hurt?"

"No. More by luck than anything else." I settled on the edge of the desk.

"What was it?"

"Roland."

"And Roland is..."

"Eliza's familiar. I avoided the worst of his paw strikes."

"Oh! Why wasn't he mentioned in the file?"

"I'm guessing the usual Angel Force incompetence. They often underestimate familiars, since they can't have one of their own. I secretly think they're jealous."

"Is he still there?" Sage asked.

"After making his sulky introductions, he vanished."

A low, rough voice cut into our conversation. "I didn't vanish. I needed to think."

Sage's ears pricked. "Is that him?"

"Greetings again, Roland." I stretched. "Meet Sage. She's a wise old familiar who comes with a side order of grump. Are you here to attack again, or is it time to talk sense?"

"I'm not here for you," Roland said, his tone curt.

"Well, that's a shame. I was going to make you a nice cup of *Sorry I Investigated Your Murdered Witch* tea."

"Juno!" Sage snapped through the connection.

"What?" I twitched my whiskers. "My hackles have yet to settle."

"If what you say is true, then you're wasting time." Roland's tone had cooled to frost.

"I agree," Sage said. "But you could try not attacking Juno when she's the only one doing any investigating. We're here to help, and you've made a mess of things."

"I don't trust her. Or you," Roland said. "I don't know you."

"Join the club," I said. "It meets on Tuesdays. We can call ourselves the Tuesday Cold Murder Club. Nice ring to it, don't you think?"

"Juno! More focus and less sass. Roland, what do you want?" Sage asked.

"I want Eliza's secrets kept safe," he said. "This one—Juno, is it—took her journal. It's none of her business. Eliza hid that information for a reason."

"That journal could hold answers to her murder," I said. "We're on the same side, Ronny."

"Don't call me that," he growled. "If you do anything reckless, I'll—"

"What will you do? I'm a cat in exile, forced to live in a cursed village, so I have little to lose. If you hadn't vanished earlier, you'd know this. I'm here to solve Eliza's murder. Sage can help. Trust her. Trust us. We used to live in the same town. Crimson Cove. We helped Angel Force solve dozens of murders."

"I don't need your life story," Roland said. "Although... why are you here and not there? I mean, Crimson Cove. What's this exile stuff about?"

"The short version, since I'd hate to bore you with my tragic history. I saved Crimson Cove, but Angel Force messed up. They blamed me for some carnage or other and banished me here. It's the higher angels' fault. They're so unhelpfully kooky and quick to get everything wrong. They're muddle makers, and I'm here thanks to their latest muddle. The inconvenience is overwhelming."

"It was mainly their fault," Sage said, "but Juno stuck her nose where it wasn't wanted, and made the angels look foolish."

"That's easy enough to do," he said.

"True enough. At least we agree on something," I said. "Roland, will you help us? We want to find out what happened to Eliza, but we keep hitting dead ends."

"Why?" he asked.

I tilted my head. "Do you mean, why do we want to help? Or why do we keep hitting dead ends?"

"What's in it for you?" Roland's tone hardened. "Around here, people don't do that. They only look after themselves."

"For the satisfying sense of justice," I said.

"Juno thinks the angels will set her free if she solves the cold cases she found archived in the library," Sage explained.

Roland gave a short, dismissive snort. "Huh."

I narrowed my eyes. "Is that a good huh, or a bad huh? Or a that's amazing and I'll help huh?"

"It's a you're confusing, and I still don't trust you huh," he replied flatly.

"Tell us about Eliza." I softened my tone just enough to make it sound less like a demand. "Any information could be useful. We know how powerful she was, and I saw the memory she cast in her cottage showing her final few seconds. Did you help with that?"

Roland's gaze slid away, the faintest twitch of his tail betraying his unease. "I'm not sure I believe you."

I kept my voice even. "Give us a chance."

His ears went back. "I don't like you enough to share anything personal."

"If you still think we're shady after we've spent more time together, I'll let you bite me," I said. "But we need everything you've got on Eliza if we're to stand a chance of solving her murder after so many years have gone by."

Sage's voice came through the snow globe. "What's he doing? I don't see him. Has Roland gone again?"

"I'm thinking!" Roland snapped. "It's been a while since I've been around other familiars. I kept out of everyone's way since Eliza died. I get looked at weirdly because I'm alive, even though she's gone."

I studied him. "Take your time. You must be strong to survive, even though your bonded witch is dead."

"Just not too much time," Sage said. "Some of us are busy."

I rolled my eyes. "Ignore Sage. She gets grumpy if she misses a nap."

"When you're this old, you're allowed as many naps as you like," Sage retorted. "Go on, Roland. Tell us about Eliza."

Roland huffed out a wheezy breath. "A lot of people feared her. They knew nothing. Eliza wasn't just my witch. She saved me. Raised me. We bonded like warm butter on a hot kipper. We knew each other's thoughts before they even formed."

Something in my chest tugged at my heart. "That's... yeah. I get it."

"You do?" Roland's ears angled forward. "You have a witch?"

"Zandra Crypt is my witch." Warmth slipped into my voice. "The most wonderful witch ever to walk this earth. She rescued me when I was neck-deep in twisted dark magic. We're the perfect bonded pair."

"Zandra Crypt? From the Crypt witch coven?"

"That's the one." I lifted my chin. "It's no surprise you've heard of her. Her power is unstoppable."

Roland's tail twitched once, slow and deliberate. "That coven is no joke. Strong witches. Fierce bond magic. Something to do with demons, aren't they?"

"They run the demon prison in Willow Tree Falls."

His gaze narrowed. "Since you're bonded to such a powerful witch, why are you stuck in Badger's Haze? Shouldn't she have gotten you out by now?"

Sage cut in before I could answer. "We can't get Juno free. Everything we've tried fails. Zandra even spent a night behind bars recently because she tried to break in and yank Juno out. She got caught by Angel Force after they warned her repeatedly to stop meddling in their ruling."

"Portal spells to access Badger's Haze collapse," I said. "Translocation spells take people to the wrong place. Nothing and no one gets through."

Roland let out a low grumble. "There's some serious containment magic around you. You must have really messed with the angels for them to fix up something so airtight."

"It's a misunderstanding," I said, even though I knew that wasn't how the angels saw it. "But I won't give up trying to break free. Zandra won't stop trying either. She'd hex the moon itself to get me out. We will be together again."

Roland looked away for a moment, and when he spoke, his voice had softened. "I wish I could get Eliza back. It's too late for me, but maybe not for you if you think solving Eliza's murder will get you home. You really want to figure out who killed my witch?"

"Once I spy a mystery, I have to solve it," I said. "And I plan to dunk Eliza's grimoire journal into the well. The water magic could decode the truth. Without the words on the pages, the book is worthless."

"I told Juno it was too dangerous and it won't work." Sage's voice was sharp with disapproval. "You talk sense into her. You know the well better than either of us. This plan has failure written all over it."

Roland shook his head. "It could work. Eliza infused tiny amounts of well water into her magic. Even after all this time, there'll be some left. She had off-the-charts power. It was an honor to be bonded to her."

"Does that mean you'll help us?" Hope crept into my voice.

"I'll help," he said, with the finality of a vow. "You'll get yourself killed if you do this on your own. This is my territory, so I know how things work."

"I feel oddly safer and slightly more endangered," I said.

"Sorry about chasing you earlier," Roland said. "I thought you were stealing Eliza's treasures. I have so little left of her. That journal is important to me. She told me to protect it and to guard her home. I've not been doing so well lately. Letting things slide. It's because the magic is fading. My power is leaving me. I don't think I have long left, but I want to do this last thing for Eliza."

His words hung between us, heavy as storm clouds. I studied his face, the stubborn pride still there under the exhaustion. A cat guarding the last of his witch's memory. And now, maybe, guarding me too.

"I'm also sorry about the misunderstanding." I dipped my head slightly in a gesture of truce. "And I'm happy to help you complete this final task for Eliza. She'd be proud of you."

"Just don't drop the journal! That well is deep, and there are water spirits in there. Ghosts, too. So people say, anyway. I never saw one. Eliza always showed the well respect."

I tucked my paws neatly under me, tail curling close. "I'll be careful. And tonight, we'll get answers."

Sage's voice crackled from the snow globe. "Be careful. Both of you."

I met Roland's gaze. "We've got this. Right, Ronny?"

His whiskers twitched in irritation at the nickname, but there was a flicker of amusement in his eyes. "If we don't, we'll go down hissing."

"That's the spirit." I rose to my paws. "Let's reveal the truth and make Eliza proud."

"And maybe shake Badger's Haze to its creepy little core," Sage added.

"Wouldn't that be lovely?" I said, although deep inside, I tingled with an uneasy certainty that the night ahead would be anything but lovely.

Chapter 12

Our adventure to the well began just after darkness fell with its usual damp, gray, unwelcome aplomb. The streets cleared fast. Lights doused. Windows bolted. The silence that followed was thick, like the whole place waited for something bad to step out of the shadows.

That was our cue. We weren't the bad, but we were on a mission that couldn't wait any longer.

Roland joined me outside the library as a plump moon peeked from behind a thick cloud. A satchel with Eliza's journal inside was strapped tight to his back. He looked like a tiny, brooding mercenary and just needed a set of throwing blades to complete the look.

We moved fast. Stealthy. Down winding alleys slick with moss. Every creak of a shutter made my murder mittens itch. Roland kept sniffing the air, his tail twitching like a metronome of anxiety.

"I smell binding wards," he muttered. "New ones. Something's reinforcing the perimeter."

"Of Badger's Haze or the well?"

"The village. Someone's scared of something in here."

"That'll be Angel Force. Those pesky feathers are determined I won't get free. Ignore their magic. We can't get distracted."

The well sat in the center of the village. Moss-covered stones, a twisted wooden frame, rope so frayed I wouldn't hang a curtain with it. But the air pulsed with old magic, so I knew the illusion of decay was just that.

I peered into the dark shaft and couldn't see the bottom. The rope was tied to a battered wooden bucket that looked like it would disintegrate if you so much as breathed on it. At first glance, I couldn't trust anything about this well.

"Are we going down in that bucket?" I asked.

"You are," Roland replied. "You're smaller."

"You're the one with the murder fangs. And the magic. You can better defend yourself when the ghosts attack."

"They won't attack. Probably." He shrugged the satchel off and nudged it toward me. "Just don't drop the journal or I'll make you dive in to get it out."

I tied the satchel tightly across my back and tugged on the rope. It groaned like a dying beast. Not confidence-inspiring, but it was all for show.

"I'll lower you," Roland said. "Don't look down."

I grabbed the rope and braced myself. Roland's paws worked quickly, lowering me inch by inch into the cold, damp shaft. The stone walls glistened with moisture. The smell of earth and stagnant magic clung to everything.

Then something moved below. Just a ripple. A shift in the shadows. But enough to freeze my guts solid.

"Roland?" I called out. "Are you seeing anything from up there?"

"Not a thing. Do you want to continue?"

"Yes, but get ready if something attacks."

I went lower. Ten feet. Twenty. I saw the shimmer of water, then something brushed my paw, causing me to yelp.

"What's wrong?" Roland shouted. "You'd better not have dropped Eliza's journal."

"Something touched me! It was slimy. Squishy. I'm not a fan of either." I tightened my grip on the rope as a cold tendril wrapped around my leg and tugged. It felt like the mighty tentacle of a ghost kraken. "Roland! Pull me up."

Before he could respond, I was yanked downward so hard the rope snapped from my paws, and I hit the water like a stone.

Panic is wet. That's the best way I can describe it. It fills your mouth, your ears, your brain. I kicked, claws scraping against something fleshy. Whatever it was, it wanted me under the water.

But I wasn't going quietly. I twisted, roared, kicked hard, and my paw hit something sharp. The thing hissed and jerked away, but not before it clawed down my leg, slicing through fur.

I surfaced gasping, coughing, sputtering spells I barely remembered, and that wouldn't work thanks to my lack of power. The journal, still strapped to me, thank the moon, glowed faintly.

"Juno! Are you dead?" Roland's voice echoed down the well's shaft. "I'm coming. Hold on."

"I'm alive. Just," I croaked. "I'm in the water, so the journal is getting a solid dunking, and it's already glowing. The plan is working."

Something hissed again, closer now. I didn't wait. I ripped the satchel open, pulled out the journal, and shoved it all the way under the water.

A blast of light erupted like a starburst, so bright I couldn't see. Magic rippled through the well. The water churned and threw me back, and I hit the wall, went under, and flailed.

Then something grabbed me again. What was wrong with this icky well beast? This time, I fought with my teeth. I bit whatever it was. Hard.

It howled and vanished into the depths.

The journal floated beside me, now glowing gold, its pages fluttering open as if wind whipped through them.

A moment later, Roland dove in with a splash and a hissed curse, causing me to go under and inhale water. He yanked me up by my scruff. So undignified.

Roland shoved me toward the rope and bucket. "Climb. Don't worry about the journal. I'll bring it with me."

I wasn't arguing. I scrambled up like a panicked tree rat, murder mittens slipping on the wet rope but refusing to give up. Roland followed close behind, his fur slicked back, eyes blazing.

We collapsed at the top, panting, soaked, shivering. The journal lay between us, wide open, the once-invisible ink gleaming. Names. Dates. Spells. Secrets written in Eliza's hand.

"Oh, wow! This is something else. Eliza always kept her words hidden, even from me. This could change everything," Roland whispered.

I nodded, still shaking from the cold and shock. "Whatever killed her, whatever she found out that led to her death is right here on these pages."

Roland flopped onto his belly, gaze glued to the words. "And now they'll come for us."

"Who?"

"They! Whoever's secrets Eliza wrote about. She was always writing in this journal."

I bared my fangs. "Let them. We'll be ready. You want to see her killer brought to justice, right?"

"I'm in. Whatever it takes." Roland stayed face down on the mossy stones beside the well, water dripping from his whiskers in a steady rhythm. His chest rose and fell in slow, deliberate pulls of air.

He wouldn't admit it, but he was hurting. Not a physical pain, but it went soul-deep. It wasn't just that he'd lost his witch, but he was unmoored. I felt it in every flick of his tail, every clenched paw, like he was holding the world together with pure stubbornness.

I knew that feeling.

I shook out my fur, sending cold droplets flying, and kept one paw hooked protectively over the journal. "Will you make it back to the library, or should I drag you by the scruff?"

A low rumble vibrated in Roland's throat. "You could try."

"Come stay with me," I said. "The library leaks, and the ghosts rearrange the books, but it's dry enough and the company's tolerable."

He finally looked at me, his eyes glassy with fatigue. "Are you offering me a place to stay out of pity?"

"Out of strategy," I said. "I need backup, and you need a roof over your head. It seems like a fair exchange."

He let out a long, shuddering breath. "Fine. But it's only temporary. And I'm not chasing the ghosts away."

"Good," I said. "They were there first."

Roland gave a small grunt, the kind that might one day grow into a laugh if he let it. "I'm exhausted. I'm not used to this."

"We can rest when we get to the library." I glanced down at the journal. "In the morning, we'll see if this thing is ready to talk."

The well gurgled behind us, sending up a breath of cold, magic-laced air. I shivered, not entirely from the chill. Somewhere in these pages was the truth about Eliza, and tonight we'd dragged it one step closer to the surface.

Chapter 13

The next morning, the snow globe shimmered on the desk, its misty light spilling across the library desk.

I tapped the glass with a paw. "Sage, are you there? We have news."

Her familiar face flickered into focus, distorted by the curve of the glass. "I'm here. And I'm happy to see you're still breathing. The well didn't eat you?"

"We did it," I said. "We dunked Eliza's journal. My leg looks like it went through a cheese grater, but it worked. The invisible ink is now very visible."

Roland was sprawled beside me on the table. "Something tried to eat Juno. I saved her."

Sage's eyes narrowed. "Juno, you said you'd be careful."

"Plans change when monsters grab your paws. But we're fine. Really. And the journal..." I nudged it forward. "It's incredible. Eliza was tracking something big."

Sage leaned closer. "Define big."

"Like the entire village is at risk big."

Roland's ears angled back. "Eliza documented everything. Names, dates, spells. The village has been bound under some kind of enchantment for decades."

"That's why so few people leave Badger's Haze," I said. "It's not tradition. They physically can't. The wards keep everyone penned in."

Sage made an indistinct sound. "Badger's Haze is broken. Only real troublemakers get stuck there. Oh, sorry, Juno. I didn't mean—"

"It's fine. We all know I'm innocent," I declared. "Just wrongly banished. Once we solve this case, everything will be fine."

She huffed, not looking convinced. "So, what's the plan now? Did anyone see you messing about in the well last night? If Eliza was killed for what she discovered, they could come after you next."

"Roland said the same," I replied. "But no, we were alone. Let's focus on the positive. Maybe with Eliza's notes, we can break whatever spell is holding the villagers. That might win me some brownie points, or at least get people talking to me."

Sage lifted a paw on her side of the globe. "Let me see the journal. Hold it up."

I balanced the book between my front paws, turning it toward the glass. "Look at this page. It's a map of the village with markings around the perimeter. Eliza called them anchor points."

Sage's eyes darted over the image. "Those look like binding runes. Old ones. There are books about them in the restricted section of Vorana's bookstore."

Roland's whiskers twitched. "I know those places. I've been to them. Those marks always smell wrong. Like something burned but still alive. They've been there as long as I can remember."

"If these are what I think they are," Sage said, "they're powered by sacrifice. Regular sacrifice. This is dark magic."

"It gets worse." I flipped through a few pages. "Look at these names. The last one is Eliza's."

Sage stared at the list. "Is that a murder list?"

Roland's ears flattened as he studied the list in the journal. "It can't be. Some of these people are still alive. Maybe it's a suspect list. Eliza was trying to find out who was messing with the village."

"Eliza wouldn't put herself on her own suspect list." I tapped a paw against the page. "There are dates next to some of these names. Maybe that's when they were supposed to be sacrificed."

"Not by Eliza," Roland said quickly.

Sage's voice crackled faintly through the snow globe. "Can you be sure? Did she tell you everything?"

"Always!" Roland said. "We were bonded. We kept no secrets from each other. A familiar who hides things from their witch is the pits. I spit on them. I grind them beneath my paw."

"Sometimes, keeping the occasional secret is good for everyone," I said.

"Oh, here we go," Sage sighed.

"I'm just saying," I went on, "not every secret kept is bad."

Roland snorted. "Says the exiled familiar who can't cast a spell."

"You said Eliza didn't let you read her journal," I countered. "That's secret keeping."

His gaze sharpened. "Keep talking if you want me to chew on those ears."

I flicked my tail. "Moving on..."

"Eliza could have trapped everyone with dark magic," Sage said. "Maybe she was planning more killings, but the magic turned on her, and she became the sacrifice."

Roland's hackles rose. "I hate that idea. Worst idea ever. You got it all wrong. I thought you said this mangy old familiar was wise?"

Sage bristled. "Watch your manners! You two need to—" She froze. "Wait. What's that sound?"

"What sound?" My ears swiveled.

"Like a scratching," Sage said. "It's coming through the globe, isn't it?"

I listened. The fur along my spine lifted. "That's not coming from our end."

Roland's head tilted sharply. "No, I hear it too. It's getting closer. And... my ears are ringing."

I stepped toward him. "Roland, are you okay? You look weird."

"I feel—" He stopped. Completely. His body went rigid, tail stiff, eyes unblinking.

"Roland?" I circled him, my voice rising. "Hey. Give me a sign that you're not in any harm."

"Not Roland." His voice was low and feminine, threaded with something ancient and cold.

Sage's image wavered in the globe. "What did he just say?"

"Not Roland. Vessel temporary. Need to speak."

"Oh, sweet mother of mice," I whispered. Roland's pupils had gone molten green, burning with an inner light that made my fur bristle. "Sage, I think he's possessed."

"By who?"

"Eliza here," the voice said through Roland's mouth. "Little time."

Sage's voice sharpened. "Juno, is that Eliza's ghost?"

I swallowed. "Eliza? If that's you, where did you hide your grimoire journal?"

"Under house. Safe space. Guarded by Roland and wooden moths."

Sage hissed, "Back away from the possessed cat. You don't know what you're dealing with, and without magic, that thing could flay you and have you for lunch."

"I'm taking the risk." I stepped closer, feeling an unnatural heat radiating off him. "Greetings, Eliza. What happened to you?"

"Murdered. Research discovered. Tried to destroy my journal."

Sage cut in, "Are you binding the village? Stopping people from leaving?"

"Not me. Harvesting power from trapped souls. Unable to leave, even in death."

"Where are they trapped?" I asked. "In the well?"

"Yes. My essence trapped, too."

A cold knot twisted in my gut. "That's horrific."

"Listen carefully," Eliza said. "Five anchor points. Must break them at the same time."

Sage leaned so close to the glass I thought she'd topple through. "Five points. Hold on. Juno, you showed me a picture in Eliza's journal. It had five points. Anchors."

"Use spell of innocent. My blood in vial. Hidden..."

"Hidden where, Eliza?" I asked.

Roland's head jerked up, his eyes burning with that unnatural green glow. "Behind loose stone. Samuel's fireplace. Left side. My blood. Willingly given. Counterspell in journal. Page forty-three."

"Let me see. Is that the right page?" I asked. "It looks like a poem about roses."

"Code," the strange voice replied. "Real spell hidden. Need five catalysts. Five places. Same time. Smash magic."

"Why hide your blood in Samuel's house? Were you close?" I asked.

"Last place anyone would look. Good hiding spot."

Sage's tone sharpened. "Five catalysts? Do you mean five people who must break the binding spell simultaneously and stop this plan?"

"Yes. Trusted five."

I swallowed. "Who are the five?"

"You. My Roland. Find three more. Trust no one over thirty summers old. Weakness in binding three days from now. Moon eclipse."

"An eclipse? Are you sure?" I asked. "I monitor the moon, and no eclipse is forecast."

"Hidden event. Forced by magic. Will perform great sacrifice."

A cold ripple ran down my spine. "Great sacrifice? How great are we talking?"

"Entire north quarter. Children first. Always the innocent first. Their power is untapped."

"That's dozens of families. Hundreds of people." Sage's voice cracked. "Badger's Haze isn't full of model citizens, but we can't let that happen."

I nodded. "We have to stop them."

"Three days. Prepare. Find three more. Protect my journal. Running out of—" Roland's body shuddered.

"Eliza?" I leaned forward, my tail lashing. "Eliza, what is it?"

"Danger coming. They sense me. Must go."

"Juno, what's happening?" Sage asked, her voice tight.

"He's convulsing!" I pressed a paw against Roland's chest. "Roland! Come back. I think he's dying. Look at me."

"Is he okay? He looks dead. Is he dead?" Sage asked.

"He just collapsed," I said, feeling the steady rise and fall of his breath. "Eliza leaving his body made him faint."

Roland groaned and cracked one eye open. "Ugh... my head. Why am I on my side?"

"Phew! You're back with us," Sage said. "I always hate to watch a familiar die."

"Die?" Roland frowned and pushed himself up onto shaky legs. "Why are you looking at me like I grew a second tail?"

"He doesn't remember?" Sage asked.

"Apparently not." I met Roland's confused gaze. "Eliza spoke through you."

Roland's ears twitched sharply. "What? That's not possible. I'd know if my witch hijacked my body."

"Well, it happened." I met his gaze levelly so he could see I wasn't joking. "And we have news. We have only three days to save the village and solve your witch's murder."

His whiskers stiffened. "What happens in three days?"

"A forced eclipse and a mass sacrifice," Sage said. "You'll not be getting much sleep until this giant tornado of evil has whipped through Badger's Haze."

"Eliza hid a vial of her blood near a fireplace in Samuel Greene's house," I said. "We need to get it and then find three people under the age of thirty to help us break the binding spell that's trapping residents and forcing them into this sacrifice."

Roland smacked his lips together. "My mouth tastes like ectoplasm. Is that a thing? Did Eliza really speak through me? I didn't know she could do that. Will she do it again? Did she ask about me?"

"Focus, Roland," Sage snapped. "This is serious. We need a plan of action."

"I can't believe Eliza possessed me," he muttered, shaking himself from nose to tail. "My fur feels wrong. Like someone brushed it the wrong way."

"Groom later," I said. "We need to get to Samuel's house and find that blood."

"Wait until nightfall," Sage warned. "You never barge into a magic user's house in broad daylight."

I hesitated, then nodded. "We need to look over the journal. And I need a nap and snacks before we go on our next mission. Seeing Roland possessed was a shock."

Roland's eyes narrowed. "Imagine how I feel."

"Where does Samuel live?" Sage asked.

"He has a house on the edge of the north quarter," Roland said.

Sage's fur bristled in the globe's hazy light. "If what Eliza said is true, that area is marked for sacrifice. Samuel will be a victim."

"All the more reason to hurry," I said. "We'll go tonight."

Roland hesitated. "Samuel can't be involved. His magic went wonky years ago. They say his house is more spirit than structure now."

"Then I may need more than nine lives for this mission. Let's review Samuel's statement. It could let us know what we're in for." I tapped the journal with a paw. "Sending it to you, Sage. And I'm adding the page Eliza mentioned, the one with the rose poem. That'll come through first."

Page 43 of Eliza Thorny's Journal

Thorns for the Rose

Break not the bloom, though its petals
are red
Circle of thorns where her memory is
wed
Scatter the soil where her soft roots
once grew
Light on the blade that still carries the
dew

Call to the wind that once tangled her
leaves

Storm through the silence of sorrows
she grieves
Burn down the altar where offerings lie
Chains made of whispers, undone by
the sky

Raise now the stone from the cavern
below
Stone is the promise no dark hand shall
know
Drown out the chant with the tides of
the deep
Flame finds no victim, nor promise to
keep

ANGEL FORCE: WITNESS STATEMENT
CASE FILE: #83-1104
SUBJECT: GREENE, SAMUEL
INTERVIEWER: ANGEL BISHOP
LOCATION: BADGER'S HAZE COMMUNITY CENTER

ANGEL BISHOP: For the record, please state your full name and occupation.
GREENE: Samuel Greene. I've been the well's sworn caretaker for thirty-eight years.
ANGEL BISHOP: And you discovered Eliza Thorny's body?

GREENE: Terrible business. Just terrible. I never thought I'd see such a thing at my well.

ANGEL BISHOP: Your well?

GREENE: Badger's Haze well. That's what I meant. That well will still stand when I'm a pile of dust. But I've been its keeper longer than most folks have been alive in this place. It feels like mine some days.

ANGEL BISHOP: Tell me exactly what happened this morning.

GREENE: I arrived early. The sun was just lifting. I like to start before the rest of the residents wake. And the well needs tending when it's quiet. Magic flows better that way. Less interference. It's not just any well. It has power. I could tell you some tales about that well. Some of the stories would turn that hair of yours white. Just like those wings.

ANGEL BISHOP: Please continue with what happened when you reached the well.

GREENE: I came with my tools. My special herbs for the monthly cleansing. As I approached, I noticed something near the well. I got closer, and there she was. Poor Eliza. Lying there all strange-like. Not natural. Her eyes were wide open. Looking at nothing.

ANGEL BISHOP: Did you touch

anything at the scene?

GREENE: No, sir. I checked for a pulse, but she was cold already. Then I ran to Angel Force to get help. Well, I say, ran. These old bones are creaky and don't like moving fast, but I got to you as quick as I could.

ANGEL BISHOP: You said Eliza was lying all strange-like. What did you mean?

GREENE: Arms out. Like this. Her fingers pointed toward the well, almost like she were reaching for it. And her face was peaceful but surprised, if that makes any sense.

ANGEL BISHOP: Did you notice anything unusual about the well itself?

GREENE: The water was wrong.

ANGEL BISHOP: Wrong how?

GREENE: Still. Too still. It usually has a bit of movement, even on calm days. That morning, it was like glass. And cold. The air around it was freezing, even though it wasn't that cold of a night. I mean, Badger's Haze isn't known for its balmy conditions, but this morning it was unnaturally chilly on that spot.

ANGEL BISHOP: Were there signs someone had performed any rituals or magic?

GREENE: There were marks. Chalk marks on the stones. Red candle wax. I know ritual signs when I see them.

ANGEL BISHOP: Because you perform rituals there yourself?

GREENE: Only ever maintenance rituals for the well. That's a different thing entirely. I keep the water and magic balanced. That wasn't what Eliza was doing.

ANGEL BISHOP: Do you know what she was trying to do?

GREENE: Not rightly. But it wasn't proper. Mixing things that shouldn't be mixed.

ANGEL BISHOP: What things?

GREENE: Elements. Fire and water. That's what I heard anyway. Bartholomew was complaining about it last week. He said she was meddling. He's just jealous. He wants the well all to himself.

ANGEL BISHOP: When was the last time you saw Eliza alive?

GREENE: Maybe three days ago? She came by the well and was taking measurements. Writing things in her little book. She was always doing that. I told her the well don't like to be snooped on, but she laughed at me. She never took me seriously.

ANGEL BISHOP: Did you say anything else to her?

GREENE: I warned her to be careful. The well don't like being studied. It's got its own rules. If you don't respect the rules, you get in trouble.

ANGEL BISHOP: Where were you before you went to work at the well?

GREENE: Home. With Martha, my wife.

ANGEL BISHOP: Mr. Greene, didn't your wife pass away three years ago?

GREENE: Oh! Right. Right. I forget sometimes. I still talk to her, even though she's gone. I meant I was at home. Alone. No one to confirm, I suppose. Well, I think Martha is still in the house. When I talk, things move. It comforts me to know she's still here, even though I can't see her.

ANGEL BISHOP: She's haunting you?

GREENE: Maybe. I hope it's Martha. It's the only ghost I want haunting me.

ANGEL BISHOP: I'll have someone check if there's a presence in your house. Ghosts can be helpful if they're strong enough to speak. What time did you go to bed?

GREENE: Nine o'clock. I'm an up with the lark type of person, so I get my head down early.

ANGEL BISHOP: And you didn't leave your house until...

GREENE: 5:30 this morning. Straight from home to the well.

ANGEL BISHOP: Were you aware that Eliza planned an experiment at the well?

GREENE: There were rumors she was up to something.

ANGEL BISHOP: Have you ever tried to control the well magic or use it for your benefit?

GREENE: No, sir. I respect it. I work with it. There's a difference. Eliza and Bart don't respect the water.

ANGEL BISHOP: Bartholomew Winters?

GREENE: He's a water witch, and good at what he does, but cocky with it. His family has watched the well alongside mine for generations. The well needs guardians and a cleaner. It always has. His family handles the water magic, and mine handles the repairs.

ANGEL BISHOP: Did Bartholomew have any reason to want Eliza dead?

GREENE: They argued about her dabbling in water magic. It wasn't her element. But kill her? No. Bart respects magical boundaries too much.

ANGEL BISHOP: Is there anyone else who may have been troubling Eliza?

GREENE: It's hard to say. I keep my head down. I don't like trouble.

ANGEL BISHOP: Did you have any issues with Eliza?

GREENE: No. I respected her work. Fire magic is a fine art. It was only when she started messing with water that I got concerned. But these young ones, they think they're immortal. I suppose I was the same when I was that age.

ANGEL BISHOP: Were you concerned enough to stop her?

GREENE: I warned her to be careful, but that's all. I told her the well was dangerous during certain moon cycles and mixing elements would backfire.

ANGEL BISHOP: One final question. In your opinion as caretaker, is there any chance Eliza's death was an accident? An experiment gone wrong?

GREENE: More than a chance. The well protects itself. It always has. You push too hard, try to take more than it's willing to give...

ANGEL BISHOP: And it pushes back?

GREENE: With consequences. I've seen it before, and I'll likely see it again. Some lessons have to be learned the hard way. It's a shame. Eliza was a powerful witch.

ANGEL BISHOP: Thank you for your time. Please remain available for further questioning.

GREENE: I'm not going anywhere. The well needs me now more than ever. An unscheduled death will have unsettled it.

BISHOP'S NOTES: The subject appears distressed by the discovery of Eliza's body, but shows signs of confusion. His alibi remains unverified, and inconsistencies in his statement about his deceased wife warrant a mental state evaluation. Arrange for a paranormal investigator to visit Mr. Greene's house and contact any house ghost, possibly his late wife, to determine an alibi.

Chapter 14

After our snow globe chat with Sage ended, I reviewed Samuel's statement, checking to see if a paranormal investigation had taken place. Sure enough, there was a record. It proved he had an alibi for Eliza's murder, thanks to his late wife's ghost being cooperative. There was also a note to say she was one of many ghosts living with Samuel.

Our next move was to visit Samuel's house to find Eliza's hidden vial of blood. Simple enough in theory.

We waited until dark, when most of the villagers were tucked away behind locked doors and warding charms. The streets were empty as we hurried along, eerily silent except for the occasional hoot of an owl or rustle of night creatures in the underbrush.

Samuel's house sat on a hill overlooking the north quarter, a crooked three-story building. Its windows were different sizes, the roof sloped at odd angles, and the entire structure seemed to lean to the left, as if perpetually caught in a strong wind.

"Are we really doing this?" Roland whispered as we crouched behind a large rock at the base of the small hill.

"Unless you want a mass sacrifice to happen, yes," I said.

"Don't forget Eliza, though. That's the only reason I'm helping. You said you'd find her killer."

"Her death is linked to all of this. Uncover the person planning to sacrifice a quarter of Badger's Haze, and we find out who killed your witch."

Roland grunted, which I took as a sign he understood these things couldn't be rushed and he'd follow my lead.

The approach to the house was easy. No guard gargoyles, no wards we could detect. Just a winding dirt path overgrown with weeds and mushrooms that glowed faintly blue in the moonlight. I tried not to step on them in case they screamed or exploded.

"The chimney is on the east side," Roland said. "It's huge, so we can climb down it. If we circle through the garden—"

"Wait," I interrupted. "Look at the windows."

Every window was open. Wide open on such a chilly night.

"That's not suspicious at all," Roland said. "Is he inviting trouble in?"

"Maybe Samuel likes fresh air?"

"Or he's expecting visitors."

"Or he's keeping them open in the hope the ghosts will leave. According to that report from the paranormal investigator, his dead wife isn't the only spirit who floats around those hallways."

We debated for approximately three seconds before deciding an open window was more appealing than scaling the side of the house to reach the chimney and scrambling down it.

We slunk through the tall grass, keeping low, until we reached a window. It was just high enough that we needed to climb onto a rain barrel to peer inside.

The room beyond was dark, but I could make out furniture. A desk, some bookshelves, and what looked like a large armchair.

"It's the study," Roland whispered.

I went first, landing silently on the hardwood floor. Roland followed with a soft thud. The moment his paws touched the floor, every candle in the room blazed to life.

We froze, waiting for shouts or magical alarms, but there was only silence.

The study was larger than it appeared from the outside, lined with crowded bookshelves and objects under glass domes. A massive desk dominated one end, covered in open books and dried herbs. And there was a fireplace. An enormous stone structure with a mantle carved with symbols.

"Left side," I reminded Roland. "Eliza said the loose stone was on the left side."

We approached the fireplace cautiously. The grate was cold, with no signs of recent use. The surrounding stonework was old, cracked in places. I ran my paw along the left side, feeling for loose stones.

"Anything?" Roland asked.

"Not yet. There are so many... wait." My claw caught on something. A small stone, no bigger than my paw, shifted slightly under pressure. I pushed harder, and the stone slid inward with a grating sound that seemed impossibly loud in the quiet house. Behind it was a small, hollow space.

"Is that it?" Roland peered over my shoulder.

I pulled out a tiny glass vial sealed with red wax. Inside was a dark liquid that pulsed with its own inner light. "This must be Eliza's blood."

"Let's go," Roland said. "We got what we came for."

I tucked the vial into the little pouch I wore around my neck.

We turned to leave and found our exit blocked by a large bookshelf.

"Let's try the door." Roland nudged me toward the study door.

I reached it first, rising on my hind legs to bat at the handle. It turned easily, and the door swung open to reveal a long, dimly lit hallway.

As we stepped through, the door slammed shut behind us with enough force to make us jump.

"This is fine," I said, my voice higher than usual. "Totally normal haunted house behavior. It's just the ghosts doing what all good house ghosts do."

The hallway stretched before us, lined with doors on both sides. At the far end, a staircase spiraled into darkness. Faded wallpaper depicted a forest scene of trees, animals, and flowers.

"Juno, the animals in the wallpaper are moving," Roland whispered. "And they have fangs."

I looked more closely. He was right. The painted rabbits hopped between trees. Birds flitted from branch to branch. And something larger moved through the undergrowth, just out of clear sight. A growl rumbled through the floor.

"Ignore it," I hissed. "We need to get to the front door. Or an open window. Just find an exit."

We started down the hallway, our paws making no sound on the worn carpet runner. The first door on the right was ajar, revealing a kitchen. The second door on the left was locked.

"Did you hear that?" Roland stopped abruptly.

I listened. From somewhere above us came footsteps. Heavy, dragging, limping footsteps.

"That must be Samuel," I whispered.

Roland shook his head. "He doesn't have a limp."

The footsteps continued, moving from overhead toward the staircase at the end of the hall.

"We should hide until it walks past." I shoved Roland toward the kitchen.

We slipped inside just as the footsteps reached the top of the stairs. Through the crack in the door, I saw a slice of the hallway and the bottom few steps of the staircase. A massive shadow appeared on the wall, cast by whatever descended the stairs. It was human, but the proportions were off, the limbs too long, the head misshapen. It couldn't be Samuel.

"What in all things nastily unnatural is that?" Roland asked.

Before I answered, a voice echoed through the house, not from the staircase, but from everywhere at once.

"I know you're here, little thieves," it said, a dry, crackling sound like fall leaves underfoot. "I smell the well water. The well always leaves its mark."

My blood turned to ice. If that was Samuel, he knew we'd been to the well. And he wasn't happy about it.

The shadow on the wall grew larger as whatever cast it reached the bottom of the stairs.

"Run! Kitchen window. Now." I turned away from the door.

We bolted across the kitchen toward a small window above the sink. It should have been open, but was sealed. I leaped first, claws scrabbling for purchase on the sill. Below me, Roland yowled in pain.

I looked back to see the kitchen floor rippling. No, not rippling. Hands were pushing through the floorboards, dozens of spectral, translucent hands, one of which had wrapped around Roland's hind leg.

I jumped back down to give him a helping paw and drag him away. More hands emerged, grasping at our tails, our paws. I bit at the one holding Roland, my teeth passing through it with a sensation like biting into ice water. It released him, recoiling as if burned by my bite.

Two more hands immediately shot up through the floorboards and seized his front legs.

I swiped with unsheathed claws, slicing through ghostly wrists that felt like congealed fog. My murder mittens came away tingling and numb, but I kept fighting.

116

Meanwhile, the floor continued to erupt with spectral limbs. Hands with too many fingers. Arms bent at unnatural angles. They grabbed at my tail, my back legs, my scruff. One even tried to cover my eyes with cold, clammy fingers that smelled of grave dirt.

"The doorway!" I shouted to Roland, who had broken free and was batting frantically at the apparitions. "If we can reach the hall—"

But the doorway was blocked by what I can only describe as a tangle of ghostly bodies.

Roland backed against the kitchen counter, his fur standing straight up. "We're surrounded!"

I leaped onto the kitchen table, thinking height might give me an advantage, but the hands stretched upward, elongating until they could reach me. One caught my hind leg and pulled. I yowled as I slid across the wooden surface, sending cutlery and mugs crashing to the floor.

"Juno!" Roland cried out. He'd made it to the sink but was being dragged back by three spectral arms.

I twisted and fought, freeing myself. That was when I noticed the ghostly figures were solidifying. What had been transparent was taking on an opalescent quality. Their faces became more distinct. Hollow eyes, gaping mouths, expressions of rage. Why did Samuel live with so many angry ghosts? It must be a horrible existence.

A large manifestation rose from the floor near the pantry. It reached for Roland. Roland hissed and spat, but was clearly running out of energy. I wasn't faring much better. My limbs felt heavy, as if the unwelcome ghostly touches drained more than just warmth from my body.

We were being herded into a corner, backs literally against the wall.

"Roland, do you have more spells? I have nothing. My magic is gone. I can only do parlor tricks."

"Nothing that works well on ghosts!" he said. "These creatures are stuck between realms, anchored by the spirit summoners in this creepy place. You see them? They're on all the walls. And without Eliza, my magic is bleak. It does no good. I could kill us if it backfires. I don't trust my power anymore."

The largest apparition was now inches from us, its mouth opening wider, revealing a swirling vortex of darkness within.

"The blood!" Roland suddenly gasped, his eyes wide with realization. "The vial of Eliza's blood, willingly given. That has all the power we need. Use it."

"We need the blood to stop the sacrifice."

"We'll stop nothing if we're dead. Do it!"

I yanked the vial from my pouch, bit off the wax seal, and splashed the contents in an arc around us. The effect was immediate and dramatic. The spectral entities recoiled with a chorus of unearthly moans, their forms dispersing like smoke in a high wind.

We scrambled back to the window. This time we made it through, tumbling into a tangle of overgrown rosebushes that scratched at our fur but felt blissfully real after the misty horrors inside.

We ran without stopping, down the hill, through the sleeping village, all the way back to the library. Only when we were safely inside, door barricaded with a chair just in case, did we collapse on the rug by the cold hearth.

"We used the blood that would have stopped the mass sacrifice. What are we supposed to do now?" I asked.

"There was no other option." Roland heaved a sigh. "It was our only way out."

"Wait! Look at the vial." Despite having emptied its contents in Samuel's kitchen, the vial was full of dark, pulsing liquid. "Blood willingly given replenishes? Did you know it would do that?"

Roland shrugged. "It's powerful witch blood. There was no one more powerful than Eliza."

"You've yet to meet my wonderful witch, Zandra. She's the most magnificent witch in the world."

He grunted again. "So magnificent, she's left you here for how long? Over a month?"

That stung. "I told you why I'm here. And she'll find a way in one day."

Roland stared at the vial. "You keep telling yourself that. Now we have the blood, let's keep going."

We spent hours checking Eliza's journal, reading and re-reading page forty-three with its poem about roses to see what secrets we could uncover.

Dawn was breaking by the time we curled up to sleep, the vial and journal hidden safely beneath a loose floorboard.

Three more people to find in a place where no one was who they seemed. Three days until the eclipse. One murder to solve. And a mass sacrifice to prevent.

It was just another week in the life of an exiled, magically blunt cat detective.

Chapter 15

We waited for the snow globe to stop misfiring. It spluttered, grunted, and possibly broke wind before connecting.

"Sage, are you there?" I asked.

Sage's voice came through the globe with its usual gruff warmth. "Where else would I be? Some of us don't have time to gallivant around haunted houses."

"You almost sound jealous," I said. "Yet you'd have grumbled and huffed the whole time if you were there last night."

Roland snorted beside me, his fur sticking up in odd tufts since he'd yet to groom all the ghostly goo off. "We nearly died. Multiple times."

"But we didn't," I said. "And we got the vial. Eliza's blood. You would not believe Samuel's house. The floors had hands."

Sage paused. "Hands?"

"Ghost hands," I clarified. "Lots of them. They clawed and grabbed and tried to drag us down to who knows where. I don't want to imagine where we'd have ended up if we hadn't fought back. I doubt it would have been the cellar where the tinned tuna is kept."

Roland shuddered. "I thought we were goners."

"And you escaped how exactly?" Sage asked.

"The blood!" I said. "We used it against the ghosts, and they scattered. But here's the weird part. The vial refilled itself. We used it all, and now it's full again."

"That's not normal witch blood behavior," Sage muttered.

"That's because Eliza was the most amazing witch to walk this planet," Roland said.

"Second most," I said.

"Third," Sage corrected. "Vorana is the best of all. My witch."

Roland rolled his eyes. "So what now? We have the vial, we have the journal, and we're still no closer to finding Eliza's killer."

"Or stopping the Badger's Haze apocalypse," Sage said.

"Is that what we're calling it now?" I asked.

"Yes! You need three youngsters you can trust for the counter-spell. And you have..."

"Two days and change until the sacrifice happens," Roland finished grimly.

"No pressure," Sage said. "Could Samuel be our killer?"

"His ghost alibi is solid," I said. "Not solid in the ghost sense, obviously, but reliable enough. There's a report tucked in the file about a paranormal investigation. The house was checked for spectral entities, and the investigator had a cozy chat with

Samuel's dead wife, Martha Greene. We didn't see Samuel, but something spooky was in the house."

"Maybe he's warped into something unstable. Guilt could have done that to him," Sage said.

Roland shook his head. "It's the ghosts. They've always troubled Samuel. After his wife died, he got into spiritualism. He spent hours talking to the other side, trying to get Martha back. In the process, he opened a portal for dozens of twisted souls, who moved in and sent him mad. Martha is there, but there's only so much she can do to keep the place from collapsing in on itself."

I sighed. "I'm sorry that happened to him, but we have to focus on solving Eliza's murder and stopping the sacrifice. Samuel isn't a suspect, so we ignore his plight. For now. When I have time, I'll do a cleanse and chase away the peskier ghosts. I'll start with the handsy ones."

"I vote we prioritize stopping the mass sacrifice," Sage said.

"My witch comes first," Roland said. "All I care about is finding out what happened to Eliza."

"And I keep telling you, they're connected," I said. "Whoever killed Eliza is the same person organizing the village sacrifice."

"Find the killer, find the mastermind," Sage said. Her voice carried a brisk, practical bite. "Eliza poked her nose into the wrong mystery, and someone shut her up. It ties back to the well. That was her obsession. The well sits at the heart of the plan to wipe out the village."

I pulled the case file closer. "We've read Vera Blackling's interview. She's the youngest suspect, which means she might know which under-thirty souls we can recruit for the counter-spell."

"Vera was Eliza's apprentice for years," Roland said. "I liked her. She was one of the few humans I let give me belly rubs."

"And she was one of the last people to see Eliza alive," I said. "Is she still in Badger's Haze?"

"Sure. She runs a second-hand herb store."

Sage snorted softly. "Second-hand herbs? They won't have much power."

"They're cheap," Roland said. "People around here like cheap. Where's Vera's statement? I want to read it."

"In the box under the loose floorboard," I said.

Roland hopped down, padded to the corner, and pried up the board.

I turned back to the snow globe. "I need information from Vera. She was in the perfect position to get to Eliza. There'd have been a bond of trust between them, so Eliza wouldn't have seen it coming until it was too late."

"What's the plan?" Sage asked. "You'll stroll into her store and ask if she murdered her mentor twenty years ago?"

"I have a more subtle approach in mind."

"You? Subtle?" Sage leaned so close to the glass her whiskers blurred. "This I have to hear."

"I'll tell Vera I found Eliza's list of favorite herbs," I said. "And I'm helping Roland gather them as a memorial. A living herb garden near the well, so people remember her."

"That's actually a nice idea," Sage said.

"I might even do it," I said. "It's not like I have a packed schedule. Only saving Badger's Haze from a mass sacrifice. All in a day's work."

"Which herbs?" Sage asked.

"No idea," I admitted. "Zandra never needed herbs to blast out spells. Neither did I."

"Moonflower, bloodroot, and white horse thistle," Sage said. "All three appear in binding work. The right combination could weaken a target. If Vera reacts when you mention them..."

"Then we'll know she's involved," I said. "Good work."

"It's only a theory," Sage said. "Be careful. If Vera was involved, she won't hesitate to remove a nosy cat with no magic and too much mouth."

Roland climbed back onto the desk with the file clamped in his teeth and dropped it beside the globe. "I grabbed the entire case. Did you see this small notepad wedged under the bottom flap?"

I blinked. "I missed that. What's in it?"

Roland nosed it open. Thin pages fluttered, stained with old ink and thumbprints. "Vera's notes. I remember she used to carry a stack of these. This one mentions Eliza buying blackthorn and rowan berries."

"Those are for protection." Sage's voice sharpened. "Protection against what?"

"Vera doesn't say," Roland said.

"While you two interrogate Vera," Sage said, "I'll research sacrifices and protection against them. Vorana knows someone who writes about dark ritual history. He might have something we can use to figure this out."

Roland closed the notebook. "We still need three people to help break the magic."

"One paw step at a time," I said.

Roland's tail lashed, the tip flicking like a whip. "We'll not have any paw steps left if we don't hurry. I'm not letting some stinking magic scum stop me from finding out what happened to my witch."

I turned toward the globe. "Sage, you still have a copy of Vera's statement. Go through it again. When we get back, tell me if you've found anything that seems strange."

"This entire case is strange," Sage said. The glow from her side of the connection caught in her eyes, sharp as glass. "Do not get killed."

I smirked. "Not planning on it."

Roland's low growl rolled through the library like distant thunder. "Let's move."

Chapter 16

Roland and I found Vera Blackling's store at the far end of Wicker Street, tucked between a long-abandoned pixie pizza parlor and a gloomy café. The store's windows were so thick with grime that the pale light barely seeped through, casting the interior in more shadow than glow.

Roland paused outside, sniffing the air. He pushed the door open with a paw, setting off a small bell that gave the most half-hearted jingle I'd ever heard.

The smell hit me instantly. It was a sharp blend of medicinal herbs, musty old paper, and something faintly metallic, like old coins left too long in the rain.

Inside, shelves pressed in on us, the aisles so narrow I had to sidestep to avoid knocking bottles over. Every available surface was crowded with jars, bundles of dried plants, and oddly shaped vials, all coated with a soft fuzz of dust.

Roland walked ahead, his tail held stiffly high. Too high.

"Trying to look brave?" I asked.

"Trying to make sure no one here thinks I'm prey," he replied under his breath.

"Comforting thought."

From the back of the store, a voice rasped, "If you're looking for catnip, we don't sell it."

I exchanged a glance with Roland.

We stepped deeper into the gloom. Somewhere behind the shelves, something small scuttled, and I wasn't convinced it was a mouse.

"Hello?" Roland called out, his voice steadier than I expected. "Vera? It's Roland."

There was a shuffling from behind a beaded curtain at the back, and then she appeared.

I've interrogated murderers, thieves, and charlatans, but something about this woman set my teeth on edge. She was tall and rail-thin, with silver-streaked dark hair pulled back so tightly it stretched her skin. At fifty-three years old, her face bore the lines of someone who'd spent too many years frowning, but her eyes were alert, darting from Roland and then to me with unmistakable calculation.

"Roland! I thought you were dead," she said flatly. "What brings you here after so many years?"

I stepped forward. "Greetings! I'm Juno."

Vera barely acknowledged me. "It's strange for a familiar to outlive its witch for so long. I suppose Eliza shared secrets with you that prolonged your life. Such as it is. Such as all our lives are worth in this lawless place."

Roland's ears flattened slightly. "We shared everything. And her murder remains unsolved. I can't cross over or move on until I find her killer."

I glanced at Roland. It was the first time he'd revealed that.

"And you pick now to investigate?" Vera glanced at me.

"I needed to try one more time." Roland lifted his chin. "Eliza deserves justice."

Vera moved behind her counter, putting a physical barrier between us. Her hands trembled slightly as she rearranged potion vials. "I have customers expected shortly. I always get busy around this time."

The lie was transparent. This shop hadn't seen a legitimate customer in days, possibly weeks, judging by the dust on the counter.

"We're organizing a memorial for Eliza." I jumped onto a stool.

Roland played along beautifully, his eyes downcast in practiced grief. "I thought you might contribute something. A memory, a spell component that was meaningful to her work. You were her apprentice, after all."

"Perhaps some herbs," I suggested. "Moonflower, bloodroot, and white horse thistle would be pleasant additions. Do you have any in the store?"

"A memorial?" Vera sounded genuinely surprised. "After all this time?"

"Grief has no expiration date," I said. "The herbs were some of Eliza's favorites. Do you have experience using such herbs?"

"Of course! Everyone with magic does."

"Did you ever brew anything using those herbs for Eliza?" I asked.

"Why would I? I learned from Eliza. I didn't give her potions. You know, even after all this time, I still think of her. She wasn't a perfect mentor, but she did her best." Vera's gaze drifted to a small framed photograph on the back wall.

From my position, I could make out a younger Vera standing beside a woman I recognized as Eliza. They were in a garden, surrounded by plants with peculiar blue-tinged leaves.

"Eliza was brilliant," Vera said abruptly. "The most talented elemental witch in the area. She understood the balance of light and dark magic in ways other witches could only pretend to grasp. It was instinctual in her."

"What do you think happened?" Roland asked. "You were close, so you must know who wanted her dead."

I felt the familiar prickle of magic gathering. Not the gentle, healing kind, but something sharper, defensive. Dangerous.

"I've answered that question before." Vera's voice was suddenly hard. "There's no point in going over it again. It'll only bring pain, and we have enough of that in Badger's Haze. Angel Force failed to bring anyone to justice, so you'll get nowhere but on the path to sadness if you prod this mystery again."

"But Eliza's murder was never solved," I pointed out. "And your alibi was, forgive me, rather thin. Alone at home, studying for an exam? No witnesses, no confirmation."

"What's it to you?" Vera's icy gaze slid to me.

"I want to help my new friend figure out what happened to his witch."

"Liar! I know all about you. Angel Force banished you here. Your magic is distorted. You're friendless. You're an outsider and aren't welcome."

I kept my tone level. "You shouldn't believe the rumors. But someone should have solved this case. Angel Force failed Eliza. We won't."

Her eyes narrowed. "You're not here about a memorial, are you? I'm not stupid. You asked about herbs used in binding magic. Do you think I did it? Bound Eliza to the well and left her to die?"

"We need to get to the truth," Roland said. "After all this time, don't you think Eliza deserves that much?"

Something in Vera seemed to crack. A hairline fracture in her composure. Her hands gripped the edge of the counter. "You think I don't? You think I haven't spent every day trying to understand what happened to my mentor?"

The magic in the room was palpable. The bundles of dried herbs overhead swayed. Small bottles clinked against each other on the shelves.

"We need your help," Roland said. "Please. I've waited years to understand what happened to Eliza. I won't find peace until everything is out in the open."

Vera's expression shifted, the anger momentarily giving way to fear and anguish. The magical energy wavered, the bottles settling. "Some stones are better left unturned."

"Why?" I asked. "What are you afraid of?"

Her eyes darted to the window, then back to us. "People who get noticed for the wrong reasons don't live for long in this angel forsaken place."

Roland sat back on his haunches, looking directly up at her. "Who do you think did it? After all these years of thinking about it, who do you believe killed Eliza?"

The question hung in the air between them. For a moment, I thought she wouldn't answer.

"Englebert." The name escaped Vera's lips like something poisonous she needed to spit out. "It had to be him. The man is so full of pride. He assumed Eliza would fall to her knees and be happy he chose her to be his wife."

"Why did he even propose?" I asked. "From what I know about Eliza, she was dating someone called Zaren Trooli."

"How do you know that?" Vera asked.

"I have access to the case files," I said. "Zaren was on the interview list."

Vera's mouth twisted to the side. "Poking about in that file won't lead you to a happy ending."

"Maybe not. But it might give Eliza the happy ending she deserves," I said. "Did you know about her relationship with Zaren?"

"Of course. They were on and off all the time. Eliza had a dumb moment of weakness and went on a few dates with Englebert after a fight with Zaren. Worst move ever. Englebert was certain she was hopelessly in love with him. She only did it to annoy Zaren and make him see what he was missing out on."

"Englebert must have some ego to believe a woman would marry him after dating for such a short amount of time," I said.

"The man has several ogre-sized egos squished inside that tiny body," Vera said. "When he proposed, Eliza actually laughed in his face. She thought it was a joke. Huge mistake. That refusal got her killed."

"How hard did Angel Force pursue Englebert as a suspect?" I asked.

"Barely at all," Vera replied bitterly. "His family practically owned magical law enforcement back then, especially in this area. They still have influence now, not that we've seen an angel around here in years. They're too scared to come to Badger's Haze and have declared it a no-fly zone."

"Something bad must have happened here for them to do that," I said.

Vera leaned forward suddenly. "You need to leave. I can't afford to be seen with you. Stop messing about in the past if you want any future in Badger's Haze."

"We can't go. I need answers. Is there any evidence that connects Englebert to Eliza's murder?" Roland asked.

"I've said too much." Vera waved a hand in the air, and the magic intensified again. The dried herbs twisted and danced overhead, and the temperature dropped several degrees. "This conversation is over."

"Your reluctance to help solve this murder suggests you were involved." It was a desperate statement, but Vera was hiding information.

"Get out!" Her shout coincided with a pulse of magic so dark and twisted that it made my fur fizzle.

The floor lurched, and we were propelled toward the door, caught in an invisible current. The door burst open, and we tumbled onto the street in a humiliating heap of fur and indignation.

For a long moment, we lay there, catching our breath.

I stood, giving myself a shake to settle my fur. "We can safely say Vera is hiding something."

Roland stared at the store, his gaze troubled. "That wasn't light magic she used. She must have learned the darker magic from Eliza. That's where she was headed. Eliza was so drawn to the well because it had ancient, twisted power."

"You've never said that before."

Roland slid me a glance. "I don't like to admit Eliza had faults. In my mind, she was perfect."

"I'll admit to a certain bias with my wonderful witch, too."

We retreated to the bench across the street, ostensibly to groom ourselves but really to keep watch on Vera's store. After about twenty minutes, Vera peered through the grimy window, checking if we'd gone. When she spotted us, she pulled back.

"Vera's emotional reaction was curious," I said. "Guilt manifests in many ways, but that outburst felt more like grief. Raw grief mixed with fear."

"They had a complicated relationship," Roland said.

"There was more to the relationship between Vera and Eliza than apprentice and mentor?"

"Maybe killer and victim?" Roland suggested. "Vera always said how much she appreciated having

Eliza as a mentor, but I'd catch her glaring at Eliza when her back was turned. It was creepy."

"She has no alibi for the time of the murder," I said. "Vera could have done it."

Roland grunted. He enjoyed a good grunt. "Maybe. But where's the proof? What do we do now?"

"We need a restorative nap. I landed on my tailbone when Vera tossed us out of her store."

"Shouldn't we go after Englebert? I never liked that guy. Eliza punctured his ego when she turned him down. It wasn't pretty."

"Nap first. Then, we have more interview files to review. Don't worry. We'll get to Englebert and see if he's hiding secrets from us."

"But we're almost out of time." Roland stamped a paw.

"We won't rest for long before confronting the rejected suitor with the angels in his back pocket."

"And let's not forget we need to stop a mass sacrifice," Roland said.

I nodded. There was nothing like a ticking clock with mass destruction at the end to motivate me.

Chapter 17

The snow globe connection hummed faintly on the desk beside me, its cloudy glass catching the dull light that seeped through the library windows.

Sage's voice slipped through the magic like a whisper carried on smoke. "From what you just told me, Vera has more power than the average resident. Most people in Badger's Haze sound too scared to use anything more than basic spells."

"She wasn't scared," I said. "Vera was angry. Still grieving, too. And she saw straight through the idea for a memorial."

"I still like that idea," Sage said. "How's Roland?"

I glanced at the scruffy shape curled in the far corner. His chest rose and fell slowly, but his paws twitched like he was chasing ghosts in his sleep. "Still napping. He pretends he's fine, but the grief is choking him. I'm still in shock he survived on his own for so long."

"He must have once had an immense amount of power."

"It's still there, but he doesn't trust himself to use it. I know that feeling. At least, I used to."

"Vera stays as a suspect?" Sage asked.

"She does. If she'd hidden her resentment toward Eliza and kept growing her power, she could have weakened Eliza, or tricked her, then let the well do the rest."

"I read Vera's statement again. There was nothing unusual. I also scanned that rose poem several times to unpick any hidden meaning. When the sacrifice hits, you've got to know how to use it."

"That's the plan." I glanced back at Roland. "Hey, he's stirring. I'll send through Englebert's statement, and we'll go over it once Roland's fully awake. Vera isn't the first person to mention Englebert, so he needs looking into."

The snow globe pulsed once in acknowledgment.

I dug through the file and retrieved the statement. The old paper crackled under my paws as I sent up a magical plea for the transmission to work.

ANGEL FORCE: WITNESS STATEMENT
CASE FILE: #83-1104
SUBJECT: Englebert Turgleton. Also present Mr. Aled Cheetham (lawyer.)
INTERVIEWER: Angel Bishop
LOCATION: Badger's Haze Community Center

ANGEL BISHOP: Please state your name for the record.
TURGLETON: Come now, we're friends, so you already know that. Did you enjoy my keynote speech at the fundraising gala for the new research

facility out near Pond Dwellings? Not wanting to brag, but I thought my joke about pond slime was amusing.

ANGEL BISHOP: Of course, sir. And may I say, the research facility is amazing. My friend works there. The requested information is just for our records. We must do everything by the book.

TURGLETON: Very well, let's get down to business. I'm Englebert Charles Turgleton the Third. Landowner, patron of local heritage, and custodian of Turgleton Manor.

ANGEL BISHOP: And your relationship to the deceased, Eliza Thorny?

TURGLETON: We were close. As close as a lady of her curious talents and a gentleman of my standing might allow. I admired her. Respected her. I proposed marriage to her.

ANGEL BISHOP: Was your proposal accepted?

TURGLETON: Regrettably, no. She declined. Kindly, but firmly. Eliza said she had more to accomplish before being anyone's wife. An unfortunate position, in hindsight. Had she accepted my proposal, perhaps she'd still be alive.

CHEETHAM: With due respect, Mr. Turgleton, we're not here to offer hypothetical outcomes.

TURGLETON: Quite right, old boy. Forget I said that. How's your section leader? I had drinks with her last month.

ANGEL BISHOP: She's very well. Let's move on. Where were you on the night of November 15th, through until approximately 6 AM the next day?

TURGLETON: Turgleton Manor. I dined privately and then retired to my study. I was indisposed for the remainder of the evening.

ANGEL BISHOP: Can anyone verify that?

TURGLETON: The usual staff members were present during dinner. Afterward, I dismissed them. I believe my butler, Mr. Kent, has already stated that I wasn't seen again until morning. It's not unusual for me to seek solitude. My days are hectic, so I enjoy some quiet interludes. What does the young crowd call it? Me time?

CHEETHAM: Mr. Turgleton has a medical condition that occasionally necessitates solitude. We must respect his privacy.

ANGEL BISHOP: What condition?

TURGLETON: Dear boy, I fail to see how that is relevant.

CHEETHAM: My client isn't obligated to disclose personal medical details unless legally compelled, or it is of relevance to the case. Which, I assure you, it is not.

ANGEL BISHOP: Very well. And my apologies. Let's discuss the location of Eliza Thorny's body. She was discovered near the old well, approximately eight hundred yards from your eastern boundary wall. Do you have a line of sight to the well?

TURGLETON: From an upper balcony, yes. On a clear day, one can see the entire wood and the caves beyond. It's a charming view.

ANGEL BISHOP: Did you see or hear anything unusual on the night Miss Thorny died?

TURGLETON: No. Nothing. The night was still. Frankly, had anything untoward occurred, I would have noticed. It's important to keep your finger on the pulse in this village. Is there anything else you need to know? I have a Runebound Revelry match starting in an hour and need to prepare.

ANGEL BISHOP: To be blunt, sir, something untoward did occur. You were romantically interested in the victim. She declined your proposal. You also live near the scene of her death. That makes you a person of interest.

TURGLETON: My, my. You angels are getting things in a terrible twist.

140

I'm not some lovesick boy. Eliza was fascinating, no doubt, but difficult. She kept secrets. She was always disappearing to collect herbs or consult her guides. She had her own world. I didn't belong in it. I thought we could make a life together, but in hindsight, I'm grateful she said no. A marriage to such a wild creature would have been difficult.

ANGEL BISHOP: Did you know about her magical practices concerning the whispering well?

TURGLETON: Everyone knew Eliza believed the well was a conduit for something. Power. Memory. I'm unsure how much of it was true. The well is old. Old things need to be respected.

ANGEL BISHOP: Did you ever take part in any of her rituals?

TURGLETON: No. I don't meddle with the unknown. My family has always stayed clear of that well. My great-grandfather tried to wall it off in 1892, after a string of disappearances. It didn't work. Frankly, it was one of Eliza's more tedious obsessions. She used to say it sang to her. That it was waking up. Utter rot.

CHEETHAM: Mr. Turgleton has provided his position. Unless you have evidence tying him directly to the death, we'll end this interview.

ANGEL BISHOP: Just a few more moments of your time. Did Eliza ever mention what she planned to do at the well?

TURGLETON: Only vaguely. She kept notes, I believe. She mentioned something about convergence points and energy veins. I nodded along, but I wasn't listening. It all sounded like theater to me. Eliza captivated me because of her beauty, but her mind was a tangled web of nonsense. That was deeply unattractive.

ANGEL BISHOP: Did she ever appear frightened or concerned about her investigations into the well?

TURGLETON: Not frightened. Driven. Although there was an edge to her in those final months. She was more focused than ever and distant toward me. I remember during our last conversation, she said something like: *It's almost here. I can feel it.* I assumed she meant a storm or a spell. She was always talking in riddles. Initially charming, then tedious.

ANGEL BISHOP: Did you speak to her the night of her death?

TURGLETON: No. Our last exchange was when I proposed.

ANGEL BISHOP: After she refused you, you didn't try to change her mind?

TURGLETON: Certainly not. I

accepted her decision and was content to move on. There are plenty of women in this village who would be delighted to be the next Mrs. Turgleton.

ANGEL BISHOP: Have you been married before?

CHEETHAM: That isn't relevant to this line of questioning.

TURGLETON: I'm happy to answer. It's no secret. I've been married five times. They all fell short of my expectations. Being the lady of my manor requires a diverse range of skills.

CHEETHAM: Mr. Turgleton has been cooperative, but this line of questioning needs to end.

ANGEL BISHOP: One last question. Do you believe Eliza's death was an accident?

TURGLETON: It wasn't an accident. She was too careful. Too clever. Someone wanted her dead because she was looking into things she shouldn't. We know our limits and stick to them, or we end up like Eliza. It's a shame. I heard she was frozen from the inside out. Is that true?

ANGEL BISHOP: I'm unable to release information about an active investigation. We'll provide more details on the cause of death when appropriate.

TURGLETON: I hope you find who

did this. Pass on my best to your captain. I must arrange for us to dine together before the next Angel Force ball. I'm the main sponsor again this year.

ANGEL FORCE INTERNAL SUMMARY REPORT: Mr. Englebert Turgleton, landowner and respected member of Badger's Haze, presented himself for questioning in the presence of his legal representative.

Mr. Turgleton acknowledged having proposed marriage to the deceased, Miss Eliza Thorny. He admitted she refused the proposal but expressed no bitterness during the interview.

While there is a lack of clarity about his whereabouts after dinner (his butler, when questioned, reported him as indisposed and not seen until morning), there is no evidence available to contradict this claim.

A check with Mr. Turgleton's doctor confirmed he has a twisted bowel that causes digestion issues. This adds weight to his alibi for the night of the murder.

Mr. Turgleton presents no credible

motive for murder. The refusal of a marriage proposal, while emotionally charged, isn't uncommon in society circles, and it would be uncharacteristic for a man of Mr. Turgleton's education and community reputation to respond with violence. He is a generous contributor to the regional infrastructure, including recent donations to the Angel Force Equipment Renewal Fund and the Badger's Haze Restoration Initiative.

It is worth noting that the Turgleton family has long been a stabilizing presence in Badger's Haze, providing employment and donations to vital community projects. Accusing such a figure without solid evidence would be inflammatory and damaging to public trust.

While I acknowledge the uncorroborated portion of Mr. Turgleton's timeline, I don't believe it merits further scrutiny unless new evidence arises.

Recommendations: No further action required.

Chapter 18

Roland's ears were pinned flat, his whiskers twitching. "It makes me sick. Angel Force just took Englebert's statement at face value. Did they even bother checking with his slaves that he was home?"

"Servants," I corrected. "Slavery's been outlawed."

"That doesn't mean it isn't still happening," Roland muttered.

"Englebert had Angel Force snug in his generous little pocket," I said. "With enough donations to their fundraisers, this division was happy to look the other way."

Sage's voice crackled from the snow globe. "I did some digging. Englebert still sits on the board of the Angel Force Benevolent Association. His family's been funding their extracurricular activities for generations."

"Money talks," I said. "And right now, it's saying: don't look too closely at the rich old guy with connections."

Roland's claws flexed against the floorboards. "Having his lawyer at the interview was a classic sign of guilt. I never liked the guy."

"Angel Force doesn't bite the paw that feeds them fancy shrimp appetizers at fundraising galas," I said. "I've been to a few. The food is always excellent."

"You weren't saying that when you got dunked in the cheese fountain," Sage said.

Roland turned to stare at me.

"That," I said firmly, "wasn't my fault."

"It never is," Sage said.

I stepped closer to the globe. "We need to get inside Englebert's home and see what he's hiding."

With no time to lose, Roland and I planned a break-and-enter inside the biggest, fanciest house in Badger's Haze.

We waited until nightfall before finding a place to watch the house to see what security measures Englebert had in place.

The manor was imposing. Three stories of weathered stone with tall windows and a slate roof.

"We need to watch out for wards," Roland whispered. "Englebert is a suspicious type. He thinks someone will steal his money."

"Or discover his dark, possibly murderous secrets," I replied.

"That too."

Once the darkness had settled in and the streets were silent, we did a preliminary reconnaissance by sneaking around the property, and I was relieved to find the wards patchy and inconsistent. Almost as if they'd been neglected.

We slipped along the perimeter wall until we reached a garden door, half-hidden by overgrown ivy. The lock was old, the kind that would respond to a simple unlocking charm.

Roland placed his paw against the lock and murmured a spell. It clicked open with barely a protest.

The door swung with a creak that made me tense. We couldn't afford to be caught before we'd even made it inside. We slipped through the doorway and found ourselves in what must have once been a magnificent garden room. Now, however...

"By the nine lives," I breathed.

From the outside, Turgleton Manor projected wealth and power. From the inside, it was a study in decay. The garden room's glass ceiling had several cracked panels, poorly repaired with magical seals that looked on the verge of failure. Rain damage stained the walls, and what furniture remained was covered in sheets that hadn't been changed in years, judging by the accumulation of dust.

"It smells nasty." Roland wrinkled his nose.

Beneath the scent of dust and neglect was something else. A magical staleness, like spells left to curdle.

We padded silently through the manor, from one disappointing room to the next. The grand foyer with its sweeping staircase was impressive until you noticed the worn carpet and the tarnished chandelier missing several crystals.

"It's like Englebert is pretending to be something he's not," Roland whispered as we peered into a sitting room where the furniture was arranged for visitors who clearly never came. "He's keeping up appearances."

"The question is why," I replied. "And where is he? Where are his butler and servants? The place is so quiet."

We found our answer on the third floor, in what appeared to be the only well-maintained portion of the house. A corridor led to a suite of rooms that showed signs of regular habitation. They were clean, with fresh flowers in vases.

I heard a man humming, the noise coming from behind a partially open door at the end of the hall.

We crept closer, peering through the gap. There sat Englebert Turgleton at a writing desk in his study, his back to us. He was short and broad-shouldered. His silver hair was immaculately styled, and he wore a smoking jacket of deep burgundy velvet that had seen better days but was still elegant.

Stuffed bookshelves lined the room, and a fire burned in the grate, casting flickering shadows. Small scraps of paper with messages on them were pinned to boards, stacked in piles, and even stuck to the walls.

As we watched, Englebert finished writing something on a notepad, tore off the sheet, and added it to a pile with a satisfied nod. Then he rose and moved to what appeared to be a small adjoining bathroom, closing the door behind him.

"Now's our chance," I whispered.

We slipped into the study and were immediately overwhelmed by the sheer volume of notes. Upon closer inspection, they appeared to be questions and answers.

"What's he doing?" Roland jumped onto the desk to examine the notepad.

I scanned the notes, reading some aloud softly. "Will the northern coven accept my application? Answer: Prospects are favorable if the donation increases. Question: Is the manor secure from prying eyes? Answer: Additional wards needed on the west boundary."

"This is all different handwriting. He's using automatic writing," Roland said. "Communing with spirits for answers. Maybe he's speaking to his ancestors so they can help him figure out how to turn this ruin around."

"That's why he was humming. The tone helps to summon his guides." It was a curious practice. Automatic writing was notoriously unreliable because you were just as likely to connect with your subconscious as with an actual spirit. Or a spirit would arrive, pretending to be friendly when it wanted to cause mischief. And there was no protection circle in the room, so Englebert was vulnerable.

But it gave me an idea. "Let's leave him a message." I nudged the pencil toward Roland with my paw. "Can you imitate Eliza's handwriting?"

Roland's eyes widened as he grasped my plan. "I'll leave a note and then we'll hide. Then I'll write on the pad with a distance control spell. The writing doesn't need to look like Eliza's, it just needs to sound like her."

We heard water running in the bathroom. We were out of time.

Roland took the pencil awkwardly between his teeth, which wasn't the most elegant solution, but needs must when a killer had to be unmasked.

He wrote in a scratchy script: *Englebert. We need to talk. Eliza.*

We barely had time to hide behind a large armchair before Englebert emerged from the bathroom, adjusting his cuffs. He returned to his desk, sat down, and immediately froze, staring at the notepad.

The color drained from his face. His hand trembled as he reached for the note. "Eliza? After all this time?"

I batted Roland's paw, signaling him to continue our ruse. He nodded and cast a spell.

Englebert gasped and held up the note before reading it aloud. "You know why I'm here. Tell the truth about me."

The effect was remarkable. The color that had drained from his face returned in a rush, his cheeks flaming red. "What do you want from me?"

Roland wrote again. *Questions are being asked. We'll find out what you did.*

Englebert leaped from his chair and paced the room. He grabbed the pencil, his hand shaking as he wrote while speaking the words aloud. "I did nothing. You made your choice. You chose poorly."

We watched, fascinated, as he carried on a conversation with himself, or rather, with the ghost he believed was communicating through his notepad. His breathing became labored, his movements increasingly agitated.

"You think I don't regret everything?" He shouted into the empty room. "Do you think I wanted things to end that way?"

Roland swept out another spell: *Tell me what happened that night by the well.*

When Englebert saw this message, he collapsed into his chair, his head in his hands. "How can you know? I've told no one. I'm certain you didn't see me."

Roland's paw shook as he threw out the spell again: *I know everything. I see all.*

"I... I followed you," Englebert admitted. "I would never hurt you, Eliza, but I wanted to understand why. Was it him? That fraud you thought you loved? I wanted to see you alone and talk sense into you. Somewhere you couldn't be influenced by those not worthy of your company."

Roland stiffened beside me.

"I saw you by the well," Englebert continued, lost in his confession to the ghost. "You were performing a twisted, dangerous ritual. Something dark spiraled out of the well. You laughed when you saw it. I knew then you were too broken to be saved."

He was crying, tears flowing freely down his lined face. "If you had just married me, none of it would have happened. You'd still be alive! It's your fault. Your fault!"

Roland and I exchanged shocked glances. Had we just witnessed a confession?

Englebert breathed heavily, staring at the notepad as if expecting a response. When none came, he grabbed the pencil again and wrote frantically: "Eliza? Are you still there? Answer me. Admit you were wrong, and you're sorry for rejecting me. I demand a response."

That was our cue to leave. We'd gotten what we came for. Perhaps more than we'd bargained for. Englebert claimed not to have hurt Eliza, but he'd been right there when she died. He had to be our killer.

As we crept toward the door, a floorboard creaked under Roland's paw.

Englebert's head snapped up. "Who's there? Show yourself! Eliza, is that you?" His gaze dropped lower, and that was when he spotted us. For a second, we all froze in a tableau of mutual surprise. Then recognition dawned in his eyes.

"You!" he snarled, pointing at Roland. "I know you. Have you been spying on me? You wrote these messages, didn't you? I knew it couldn't be Eliza. You scheming sneak."

I've always found that when discovered in a compromising situation, audacity was the best policy.

"Greetings! Angel Force will be interested to hear about your presence at the well the night Eliza died. It's a different story from the one you told the angel who interviewed you just after Eliza was murdered. I wonder why you lied to them? Hiding a guilty act, perhaps?"

"How dare you enter my home!" Englebert raised his hands, magical energy crackling between his fingers. "No one will believe you. And the angels care nothing about this place. They won't listen to a word you tell them."

"They might believe that." I gestured at the notepad where his own hand detailed his presence at Eliza's murder.

Englebert lunged for the notepad, but Roland was faster. He grabbed it between his teeth and leaped from the desk, darting under a bookcase where he couldn't be reached.

"Give that back, you mangy creature!" Englebert dropped to his knees and reached futilely under the furniture.

I took advantage of his position to jump onto his back and squash him to the floor. "Roland! Run!"

Roland wiggled out from under the bookcase, still carrying the notepad. I bounced off Englebert, causing him to yelp as I dug my claws in, and we escaped, heading through the manor and out through the same garden room we'd entered, Englebert's curses and shouts following us.

Only when we were safely off the property did we stop to catch our breath.

Roland dropped the notepad. "That was the most reckless thing I've ever been part of."

"Even more reckless than diving into a whispering well to save a banished cat you barely know?"

He grunted. "Maybe the second most reckless thing."

"It was effective," I pointed out. "We now know Englebert was there when Eliza died. Was he an observer, or did he have a hand in her death?"

"He was lying. Eliza would never perform dark magic."

I hesitated. "Are you sure?"

Roland looked away. "She was my witch. I loved her. I still do."

"Even the best witches make mistakes."

"Does yours?"

"Never! Well, rarely. And I'm always there to set her right."

"Not anymore."

"But I will be soon. Which is why we must solve this case."

Roland looked thoughtful. "As much as I hate the guy, Englebert sounded broken rather than guilty."

"Maybe he's broken because he's been carrying a secret for too long. Deception will eat away at a person until it becomes too much to carry."

Roland grunted again. "I don't like the guy. I don't trust him. But a killer... he'd never get his hands that dirty."

"Could he have paid someone to do it?"

"With what? That guy looks like he lost his fortune a long time ago."

We made our way back to the library, the notepad secure between Roland's teeth. I wasn't sure about Englebert, either. On the outside, he seemed influential and self-assured, but the manor was downtrodden, and the spell Englebert had sparked felt weak. Was he strong enough to kill someone as powerful as Eliza?

We needed a plan. Our next move. Before the sacrifice rolled around, and we were too late to stop it.

But what that plan would be, I was some ways from figuring that out.

Chapter 19

Snow flurried across the glass of the globe, obscuring Sage's face. Her voice came through muffled and irritated. "I see swirling snow but no cats. This thing is the worst. And where have you been? I didn't think it would take this long to deal with Englebert."

"We're here!" I tapped the side of the globe until Sage's image fuzzed into focus. "This connection is awful. It must be magical interference in Badger's Haze. Or maybe I need to kick the globe again. Sorry for the delay. Roland needed a snack and a nap before we caught up with you."

"Lies," Roland said. "Juno made us break into the butcher's shop on the way back. We stole sausages. Then we ate them, and Juno passed out."

"I had a brief sausage-induced snooze," I admitted.

"I'm glad you survived breaking into Turgleton Manor and had a decent meal," Sage said. "Did it work? Did Englebert kill Eliza?"

"Englebert confessed to being present when Eliza died," I said.

"We can't trust what he said," Roland spat. "Eliza would never practise dark magic. Never! He's lying."

"Hmmm," I murmured.

"Don't hmmm me," Roland snapped. "She was my witch. I knew her best."

Sage sighed. "We're all biased with our witches. But listen. I dug around and found a contact who might help. I'll link him into our conversation. It's Professor Busby from the Academy of Mystical History."

"What did he find out?" I asked.

"He'll tell you himself. Wait a second. The globe's being stubborn, so I'm forcing a link. Got it! Over to you, Professor. You're patched through to Juno and Roland in Badger's Haze."

A round-faced man with silver hair appeared in the globe. He cleared his throat. "Yes. Hello there. It sounds like a fascinating case you've stumbled upon. Quite fascinating indeed. Badger's Haze has a rich history of warped magic. I've published several papers about the area. It used to be an extraordinary place."

"Greetings, Professor," I said. "Your expertise is welcome, although we have limited time. Has Sage filled you in on our problem?"

"She has, quite adequately. I've been researching the history of the enchanted well where the witch's body was found. The well is much older than the village itself."

"Eliza said it predated human settlement," Roland said.

"Precisely," Professor Busby said with a gleam in his eye. "Because it's not just a well. It's a portal. Or rather, it can become one under specific circumstances."

My whiskers twitched. "What kind of portal?"

"The kind that opens to realms no sensible magic practitioner would ever want to access," Professor Busby said. "According to ancient texts, the well was sealed by the first magical settlers because what lived inside it was too hungry and couldn't be controlled."

"Hungry?" I asked.

"There's an old myth," he went on, lowering his voice, "dismissed as superstition by most modern magic users, that the portal can be reopened with the right sacrifice. A powerful witch, offered at the right moment, provides enough magical energy to break the seals and forge an entrance into realms that destabilize everything."

Roland shook his head. "Eliza wasn't a sacrifice. She was too clever and too powerful to fall for any tricks. She would have known if someone was messing with her."

Professor Busby leaned closer, his image blurring slightly as if the magic in Badger's Haze resisted the conversation. "The timing of her death was significant. It happened during the vernal equinox, one of the most potent points in our magical calendar."

Sage frowned. "But whoever killed her failed. The well hasn't turned evil. Badger's Haze might have its problems, but Juno hasn't stumbled across any open portals."

"That is curious." Professor Busby tapped his chin. "If a portal were still open, you'd know. Do you have powerful magic users in Badger's Haze?"

"We used to. Not so much anymore," Roland said.

"Most people here are stuck," I said. "Their magic's been warped or taken. We have Vera Blackling. She was close to Eliza and still has power."

"What about Englebert Turgleton?" Sage asked. "All that fortune and his ability to buy whatever he wants."

"Not Eliza's hand in marriage," Roland muttered.

"He's not as rich as he pretends," I said. "He most likely spent his money bribing angels or covens to get what he wanted, but overstretched himself."

"You don't think he killed Eliza?" Sage asked.

"I despise the guy, but he hasn't got it in him," Roland said. "My guess is he went to the well to guilt her into feeling sorry for him. Then he saw her pulling up serious magic, and he panicked. Ran off. Coward."

"Or," I said slowly, "he funneled his money into opening a portal, and he had to stop Eliza before she figured it out."

Professor Busby's eyes lit with interest. "Portals require continued maintenance. He could have been paying for that. Blood offerings, magical energy. Much like the old gods and goddesses, they need to be adored and fed, or they grow restless and misbehave."

"Juno can tell you all about that," Sage said with a smirk.

"Now's not the time," I replied.

"Could Eliza and Englebert have worked together to open it?" Professor Busby asked.

Roland flattened his ears. "Eliza wouldn't waste her time on him. She didn't respect him, and she outranked him with her magic."

"Perhaps they competed for whatever power the portal offers," Professor Busby suggested. "What about the well itself? Has anyone checked it recently?"

"I swam in it," I said. "There are things under the water that grab and bite."

Professor Busby's expression pinched. "Oh my. That sounds... dangerous. Perhaps you should leave this to Angel Force."

"They've abandoned Badger's Haze," I said. "We're in charge."

"Juno's temporarily working cold cases until she gets home," Sage added quickly. "We don't want anyone getting the wrong idea."

"Solving this case is my ticket home," I said. "Until then, Roland and I will handle things. Is there anything else you can tell us?"

"There is one last thing," Professor Busby said. "If you confirm an active portal, don't close it yourselves. Such work requires specific countermagic and dozens of trained practitioners."

"We don't have that option," I told him. "No one else cares about what's happening here, so we'll have to make do. Can you help with the three additional helpers under thirty? We need magic users to deactivate the anchor points, and we have no idea where to find them. People aren't exactly lining up to save the village."

Professor Busby's face brightened. "Oh yes. This is exciting. I haven't seen this ritual performed in over forty years. It is truly extraordinary."

I leaned forward. "How powerful do the witches need to be?"

"No, my dear familiar. You're not looking for witches at all." His eyes glinted, and the faint crackle of the snow globe connection made his voice echo. "You need three powerful familiars. Do you have any of those in Badger's Haze?"

Chapter 20

The snow globe dimmed, its glow fading as the connection snapped shut, and Professor Busby left us.

"Familiars!" Roland declared. "Why didn't I think of that? We're the only reason this village hasn't imploded in on itself."

"And with me here, things are only looking up. After all, I do solve what others can't," I said. "If Angel Force had any sense, they'd hand me a medal and let me run all of their investigations."

"They'd hand you a mop and ask you to clean up your mess," Sage muttered. "What are you sitting there for? Go find some familiars with power who don't hate you!"

Roland and I left the library full of renewed enthusiasm. The mist clung to Badger's Haze like a wet blanket nobody had the energy to shake off. The cobblestones were slick under my paws, the air heavy with the scent of damp leaves and the faint tang of wood smoke that never seemed to fade.

"I say we start with the butcher's cat," I said, trotting toward the store. "She's always sitting outside watching the world go by."

"There's power there, but not much friendliness," Roland said. "Margot spends most of her day judging everyone or licking herself into a trance."

"She's territorial and nosy. It's the perfect combination."

"You try Margot. I'll see if anyone else is about," Roland said. "I'll meet you in the square in thirty minutes."

Margot sat on the shop's doorstep, licking one paw with deliberate slowness. Her gaze locked on me as I approached, and she let out a low hiss before I could introduce myself.

"What do you want?" she spat.

"Greetings! I'm—"

"I know who you are. Go away."

"But I need your expert—"

"We don't need outsiders poking around," she snapped, her voice a sharp slice. Her yellow eyes narrowed to slits, and the tip of her tail flicked like she was counting down the seconds until she pounced. "No one wants you in Badger's Haze. Get out."

"If I had a choice, I'd be long gone," I muttered, stepping closer just enough to show I wasn't intimidated. "You'd rather let the village get swallowed by a ritual sacrifice than listen to a fellow familiar?"

"Don't lie! This place has survived plenty of disasters without you poking your snub little snout in. We don't need a cursed town cat turning up with dramatic warnings and stirring the pot just to get attention."

"You won't survive this one." I lowered my voice. "The north quarter will soon be gone. Do you want that on your conscience?"

She gave a sharp, humorless laugh. "Conscience? You don't know this village at all." Then she turned her back and disappeared through a grubby cat flap.

The next familiar I found was a scruffy calico perched on a crumbling stone wall near the bakery. The air smelled faintly of burned bread, and the street was so narrow the buildings leaned toward each other like they were conspiring.

"Excuse me," I began, trying for polite. "We're looking for a few strong familiars—"

She didn't let me finish. Her paw shot out, quick as a striking snake, and she bopped me square on the booping snooter. This wasn't the kind of boop I liked or expected.

"What was that for?" I took a step back, so I was out of paw strike range.

"For thinking I'd even consider talking to you." She leaped from the wall, landing so close I felt her whiskers brush mine. "And this—" Her claws slid out "—is for staying where you're not wanted."

I bolted, my paws slipping on the slick cobblestones as she chased me, yowling curses. Her screeching echoed off the narrow alleys, bouncing from shuttered windows and dripping drainpipes until I couldn't tell where she was.

By the time she gave up, my lungs burned and my fur stood on end. Somewhere behind me, her voice carried on the wind. "Don't come back, stranger! No one likes you."

By the time I returned to the square, my fur was ruffled and my pride dented. Not a single familiar had agreed to talk, let alone join our cause.

Perhaps my approach was wrong. No one stayed in Badger's Haze or came here by choice. They ended up here the way driftwood ends up in the shallows, after being tossed about by storms until there's nowhere else to go.

I was good at interrogation, piecing together evidence, and magical forensics, but winning trust without my magic and an Angel Force banishment hanging over my head like a farty cloud? That made things tricky. And without my spells, I couldn't force the issue.

I caught sight of Roland strolling across the square, his head high, his tail swaying in an easy rhythm that said he belonged here. Of course he did. He was a local. If the village was going to open up to anyone, it would be him.

Maybe it was time to let him lead.

I slid off the wall and fell into step beside him, my paws still stinging from the sprint. "Change of tactics. You're in charge."

He smirked. "What went wrong?"

"Oh, nothing major." I flicked a paw to shake off the rainwater dripping from the overhanging gutters. "Just got threatened, insulted, and chased halfway across the village."

"So... a standard Badger's Haze greeting, then?"

"Call it what you want. I'm done being the friendly face. You're local. They might listen to you before trying to claw your nose off."

He tilted his head. "Or maybe you've just lost your touch."

"My touch is fine," I snapped. "It's this place that's the problem. They look at me like I'm here to steal their last mouse and curse their kittens."

Roland chuckled under his breath. "You do have that look, especially now your fur is fluffy from the damp."

I stopped walking and gave him my coldest stare. "You're enjoying this, aren't you?"

"We take our pleasure where we can, but fine. I'll take the lead. And you're welcome."

I followed him toward the next shadowed alley, where another set of wary eyes watched us from a low windowsill.

In other places, my name meant something, and my reputation opened doors. But here, I was an outsider. Worse than that, I was unwanted. And the feeling was mutual. Still, I'd been the outcast before, and I'd survived. I'd survive it now. We would find those familiars. We had to. Badger's Haze depended on it.

And so did I. Every step forward brought me closer to Zandra, and the home that tugged at me like a thread of magic I could never cut.

Chapter 21

Roland was hunched at the far end of the library table, pretending to sleep, though his ear kept flicking.

I was grumpy. We'd recruited no familiars. When I'd handed the job to Roland, I figured his reputation would be the breakthrough we needed, and we'd spent hours prowling the alleys, stopping to speak with every familiar we could find.

Some had flattened their ears and stalked away before we'd finished introducing ourselves. Others scoffed at the idea of a mass sacrifice, claiming it was just another village rumor. A few looked startled to see Roland, whispering that they'd assumed he was dead since his witch had been gone so long.

By midday, we'd spoken to nearly a dozen cats and one bad-tempered ferret, and not a single one agreed to stand with us.

"Since the recruitment drive is on pause, we may as well review the final interviews," I said to Sage, who I'd been complaining to for the last five minutes.

"Let's start with Zaren Trooli. He was Eliza's boyfriend, correct?" she asked

I flipped open a case file. "Yes. I've already skimmed it, and nothing stuck out as odd. There's also Iris Montgomery. Eliza's best friend."

"Send me the statements," Sage said. "You could have missed something."

I muttered under my breath as I rifled through the papers. "Let me find them. I'm sure they were right here. I'll give you my summary of Zaren while I sort. Roland must have been moving things again."

"More lies," Roland announced without opening his eyes.

"Zaren initially downplayed his relationship with Eliza, but then Angel Force found a custom-made engagement ring in his workshop which was meant for her," I said. "He also admitted to arguing with Eliza just days before her death."

"What did they argue about?" Sage asked.

"Eliza's research." I checked under a stack of weathered parchment and frowned. "Where is that statement? I thought I'd put it back in the box. Anyway, Zaren mentioned Eliza had scheduled a meeting with Angel Force."

"But she never made it to the meeting?" Sage asked. "Because he killed her?"

"Possibly!" I hopped off the table. Maybe the papers had slid onto the floor.

"Did Zaren know what the meeting was about?"

"He claimed he didn't. Ah!" I jumped up next to Roland and nudged him. "Got them. Guess where they were?"

Sage sighed. "Surprise me."

"Roland was sitting on them!"

ANGEL FORCE: SUSPECT STATEMENT
CASE FILE #83-1104
LOCATION: Badger's Haze Community Center
INTERVIEWER: Angel Seraphina

ANGEL SERAPHINA: This interview is being recorded and transcribed. For the record, please state your full name, occupation, and relationship to the deceased.
TROOLI: Sure. Zaren Trooli. I'm a tech mage specializing in artifact restoration and enhancement. I'm, I mean, I was Eliza's boyfriend. We'd been together for eight months.
ANGEL SERAPHINA: Can you tell me when you last saw Eliza alive?
TROOLI: Two days before she... before she was found. We had breakfast together at that little café near the village square around 9 AM. We were there for maybe an hour, then she went to work, and I headed to my workshop.
ANGEL SERAPHINA: And that was the last time you saw her?
TROOLI: In person, yes. We exchanged messages later that evening. Just typical stuff. She was telling me about a rare grimoire she wanted to

buy.

ANGEL SERAPHINA: Can you describe your relationship with Eliza?

TROOLI: We were good together, but it wasn't overly serious. She was brilliant. Her knowledge of magical artifacts was unparalleled. That's how we met. I needed help to research an enchanted mirror I was restoring. The local librarian referred me to Eliza. I already knew her in passing, but that was how we got to know each other.

ANGEL SERAPHINA: Was the relationship serious?

TROOLI: We enjoyed each other's company and shared interests. We were taking things slow. Eliza focused on her career, and I respected that. I'm the same with my work.

ANGEL SERAPHINA: Several residents reported an argument between you and Eliza three days before her death. Can you tell me about that?

TROOLI: This village runs on gossip. It wasn't a big deal.

ANGEL SERAPHINA: What was the disagreement about?

TROOLI: A project Eliza was working on. It was a personal research project. I thought she was getting in too deep with her use of old magic.

ANGEL SERAPHINA: What

concerned you about the project?

TROOLI: Look, Eliza was brilliant, but sometimes brilliant people don't recognize when they're crossing lines. She'd found old texts about binding rituals. I told her it was dangerous territory, both magically and ethically. She didn't appreciate my concern.

ANGEL SERAPHINA: A witness overheard you say: 'You're messing with forces that could destroy everything in this village, including us.' Is that accurate?

TROOLI: I was worried about Eliza's safety. The magic she researched had consequences.

ANGEL SERAPHINA: Did your argument resolve?

TROOLI: Not really. We cooled down later, and she sent me a message that evening saying she understood my concerns, but she needed to follow this path. I replied that I respected her decision, but I was still worried about her.

ANGEL SERAPHINA: Did you speak again after that exchange?

TROOLI: Sure. We were moving past the argument. We didn't mention her research and talked about other things. Sometimes, it was easier to avoid the tough stuff.

ANGEL SERAPHINA: Let's go to the

day before Eliza died. Walk me through your day.

TROOLI: I woke around seven, the same as always. I had coffee at home and then worked on a commission until late evening. After work, I helped Iris with stock inventory at her store. I was there until nearly midnight.

ANGEL SERAPHINA: That's a long inventory session.

TROOLI: You haven't seen Iris's store. It's chaos. Magical items everywhere. She's brilliant at what she does but terrible at organization. I help her every month. Each item needs to be identified, its magical signature recorded, and its condition assessed. It takes time. Some items are unstable, and you can't always trust what they'll do. I designed tech that helps. It's a prototype, and I'm refining it thanks to Iris letting me test it on her stock. I hope to get it on the market by the end of the year.

ANGEL SERAPHINA: Iris can confirm you were there?

TROOLI: Yes, absolutely. We were in the same room most of the time.

ANGEL SERAPHINA: Eliza died in the early hours of the morning. Where were you at that time?

TROOLI: Sleeping.

ANGEL SERAPHINA: Alone?

TROOLI: Yes.

ANGEL SERAPHINA: And when did you hear about Eliza?

TROOLI: I got a call around 8:30. I couldn't believe it. Then I panicked. I knew immediately it wasn't an accident.

ANGEL SERAPHINA: Why would you think it wasn't an accident?

TROOLI: Eliza was too knowledgeable to mess up that badly. If something went wrong, it wasn't by chance. And the texts she studied were dark. The kind of darkness that attracts attention from entities you don't want noticing you.

ANGEL SERAPHINA: Do you believe someone or something harmed Eliza because of her research?

TROOLI: Or because of what she found out. Eliza mentioned references to something planned in Badger's Haze.

ANGEL SERAPHINA: Did she share specifics about this discovery?

TROOLI: No. She was cautious and said she needed to verify things before going public.

ANGEL SERAPHINA: Were you aware of Eliza having any enemies in the village? Anyone who might wish her harm?

TROOLI: Eliza asked too many questions, so not everyone loved her, and she could be blunt, but she had friends. I wouldn't say she was unpopular.

ANGEL SERAPHINA: What about previous relationships that ended badly?

TROOLI: Eliza mentioned an ex from her academy days, but they'd been apart for years before she moved here. I never got the impression that there was trouble between them.

ANGEL SERAPHINA: What about her relationship with Englebert Turgleton?

TROOLI: Ha! Good one. That wasn't real. Eliza was angry with me. She thought I'd flirted with someone else, which I hadn't, so she accepted Englebert's invitation to dinner. No one took that seriously. Even she found it funny.

ANGEL SERAPHINA: One more question about your relationship. You said it wasn't overly serious, yet when we searched your workshop, we found a ring.

TROOLI: How? I didn't give you permission to search my place.

ANGEL SERAPHINA: We had a warrant. It was a custom piece with moonstone and silver, which are traditional engagement materials for rings offered to elemental witches. Who was the ring for?

TROOLI: I... I lied earlier. The relationship was serious to me, but I didn't want to pressure Eliza. She was so focused on her work. And if I'm being totally honest, I was worried she'd pick the books and magic over me.

ANGEL SERAPHINA: How did that make you feel?

TROOLI: I was happy to wait. She was one of a kind.

ANGEL SERAPHINA: Were you aware Eliza had made an appointment to speak with Angel Force? It was scheduled for today.

TROOLI: What? No. She never mentioned that. What was it about?

ANGEL SERAPHINA: We don't know. She requested a meeting but didn't specify the reason. Did she ever indicate feeling threatened or in danger?

TROOLI: Um... about a week ago, I found her putting up additional protective wards around her house. When I asked why, she said she was being cautious. I assumed it was related to her research, and she was worried about magical interference.

ANGEL SERAPHINA: Did she keep her research materials at home?

TROOLI: I think so, but she never wanted me poking about. She hid her important notes and the original texts she worked from.

ANGEL SERAPHINA: Have you been to her home since her death?

TROOLI: No. I was told the scene was sealed while you investigated.

ANGEL SERAPHINA: Eliza's home has been searched. Do you have any idea who might have done that or what they were looking for?

TROOLI: No! That's disturbing. Someone went through Eliza's stuff? Did they want her research? She wasn't rich, so they couldn't have been after her money or jewelry.

ANGEL SERAPHINA: Is there anything else you think we should know? Anything that might help us understand what happened to Eliza?

TROOLI: I'm convinced Eliza's research caused her death. And there's one more thing. The night before we argued, she told me she'd contacted something in her dreams. She was excited about it, but it scared me. Dream contact is dangerous because you never know what's really talking to you.

ANGEL SERAPHINA: Thank you for your time, Mr. Trooli. We may need to speak with you again. Please don't leave Badger's Haze without informing us first.

TROOLI: I won't. I'm not going anywhere until I know what happened to Eliza.

Interviewer's Notes: The subject appeared composed. His emotional responses seemed authentic, particularly when confronted with evidence of the engagement ring. However, the initial downplaying of their relationship raises questions.

Recommendations: Obtain and review the victim's research materials and any papers of relevance not taken from the home and confirm Mr. Trooli's movements on the night of Miss Thorny's death.

Roland sat back. "Zaren wasn't serious about Eliza, but he had an engagement ring? That wasn't for Eliza."

Sage's voice came from the snow globe. "Their argument over the magic Eliza was testing could have been more intense. Binding magic is dangerous. Eliza must have known how deadly it was if she put extra wards around her home. She felt threatened."

Roland huffed. "If Zaren really loved her, he'd have done more than tell her she was in danger. He'd have stopped her. I never saw him try anything like that."

"Do you trust Zaren?" I asked.

"He never gave me a reason to distrust him, but I didn't pay him much attention. He was just another guy Eliza would get bored with and forget about. Maybe I should have been more suspicious."

I tapped the edge of the statement. "Zaren stays on our suspect list until we've got proof otherwise. His alibi is Iris Montgomery, and she's our next interview."

"Let's line it up," Sage said.

ANGEL FORCE: SUSPECT STATEMENT
CASE FILE #83-1104
LOCATIONS: Badger's Haze Community Center
INTERVIEWING ANGEL: Angel Seraphina

ANGEL SERAPHINA: This interview is being recorded and transcribed. For the record, please state your full name, occupation, and relationship to the deceased.

MONTGOMERY: Iris Montgomery. I own the Curious Claw. It's a magical artifact shop in Badger's Haze. Eliza is... was my best friend. We met when she first moved to the village. I wish we didn't have to do this right now. It's so awful. I'm still in shock.

ANGEL SERAPHINA: Take as much time as you need during this conversation. Miss Montgomery, when did you last see Eliza alive?

MONTGOMERY: Three days before she died. She stopped by my store around four PM. She wanted to show me a book she'd discovered in the library archives.

ANGEL SERAPHINA: Did you speak with her after that?

MONTGOMERY: We exchanged messages the next day. She asked if I had any references on binding rituals in my private collection. I sent her a few scans of relevant pages from a grimoire. That was our last communication.

ANGEL SERAPHINA: How would you describe Eliza's mood in the days before her death?

MONTGOMERY: Excited. Energized. She said she felt on the verge of a significant discovery. But also anxious, I think. She mentioned feeling watched.

ANGEL SERAPHINA: Did she say who might be watching her?

MONTGOMERY: No, not specifically. I assumed it was paranoia from working with older magical texts. They leave a residual psychic impression. Old magic is hard to work with. It takes concentration and time. Eliza was always so impatient to figure things out. She'd rush through the ward protections or sometimes forget to do them. I was always telling her off about that.

ANGEL SERAPHINA: Were you aware of conflicts Eliza had with anyone in the village? You mentioned she researched protection magic. Was that for a specific reason?

MONTGOMERY: We all need protecting now and again. Did you know she was interested in harnessing the well magic? Anyway, it's sensible to have a safety net around you when experimenting with power. I figured that was why she needed it. Maybe not. It could have been because she felt watched. I feel bad. I should have paid more attention to her concerns, but Eliza was so self-assured. Everything worked out for her. Well, until it didn't.

ANGEL SERAPHINA: Who might have had an issue with Miss Thorny?

MONTGOMERY: Everyone knows Eliza rejected Englebert's proposal, but you've probably spoken to him. Eliza also had issues with Samuel and Bart. They're the well's protectors. Samuel cares for the well. He loves that well. Probably more than his late wife, Martha. She was a sweet lady.

ANGEL SERAPHINA: Do any of those people particularly concern you?

MONTGOMERY: Oh! Well, I don't think it was Samuel or Bart who hurt Eliza. They disagreed with her more often than not, but it was never threatening. At least, Eliza never mentioned fearing them. She once said they were overblown windbags who should get out of her way if they knew what was good for them. Englebert, I mean, he's a proud man. Not magically strong, though, but he has influence because of his pots of money. I don't know, though. All of this is a guess, and I don't want to get anyone in trouble for making suggestions with no proof. People argue all the time.

ANGEL SERAPHINA: What about her relationship with Zaren Trooli?

MONTGOMERY: Oh! They were good together. Both skilled in their fields. They had their disagreements, like any couple, but never over anything serious.

ANGEL SERAPHINA: We've received reports of an argument between them shortly before Eliza's death.

MONTGOMERY: Yeah, that's true. At least it is if you believe the village gossip, which is usually accurate. Zaren was concerned about Eliza's research. He thought she was delving into dangerous magic. I didn't disagree with his concerns.

ANGEL SERAPHINA: Let's discuss the night Eliza died. Can you walk me through your day?

MONTGOMERY: It was a normal day at the store, not too busy. I did stock inventory that night. I do a monthly check on condition, containment, and to assess new items I've brought in before they go on sale.

ANGEL SERAPHINA: Were you alone?

MONTGOMERY: No. I never work alone with new items, just in case there's something wrong with them. Zaren came over around eight that evening to help, as he always does. His expertise is invaluable with the complex artifacts. He has this fancy gadget he waves over the unstable stuff, and it's like magic. They behave. Well, it is magic. He's great at what he does.

ANGEL SERAPHINA: And you were both at the store all evening?

MONTGOMERY: Yes, the entire time.

ANGEL SERAPHINA: Did you leave at any point?

MONTGOMERY: No. With magical artifacts, you can't walk away in the middle of an assessment. Some items require continuous attention once you start working on them.

ANGEL SERAPHINA: What time did you go home?

MONTGOMERY: Around midnight. It was a late one.

ANGEL SERAPHINA: Do you live

alone?

MONTGOMERY: Yes.

ANGEL SERAPHINA: Is there anyone who can verify your whereabouts?

MONTGOMERY: My security system logs entries. It'll show that I didn't leave home until the next morning. Why do you ask?

ANGEL SERAPHINA: When did you learn about Miss Thorny's death?

MONTGOMERY: Mrs. Kettleworth contacted me as soon as she heard the news. She knew Eliza and me were close.

ANGEL SERAPHINA: We understand you're a beneficiary in Eliza's will. Were you aware of this?

MONTGOMERY: How do you know that?

ANGEL SERAPHINA: Please answer the question.

MONTGOMERY: Oh, well, sure. It's nothing to hide. We had a conversation about it a year ago. After Eliza's parents died, she updated her will. She didn't have many people in her life she trusted. We promised to look after each other's collections if anything happened. Magical practitioners often accumulate items that need special handling. She's a beneficiary in my will, too.

ANGEL SERAPHINA: Can you

specify what you'd inherit?

MONTGOMERY: Her personal library. Books on elemental magic mostly, and a few personal effects. Her magical tools, crystals, that sort of thing.

ANGEL SERAPHINA: Are there items of particular value in her collection?

MONTGOMERY: Value is relative in magical terms. Some of her books are valuable. There's a first edition of *Starlight Bindings*, but most of the value is academic, not monetary. Neither of us has oodles of cash. We work for the love of our jobs, not for the fame or fortune. Or rather, Eliza did. I still do. You know what I mean.

ANGEL SERAPHINA: Were you aware of any dangerous or powerful artifacts in her possession?

MONTGOMERY: Nothing comes to mind. Her power was in her knowledge, not in the objects she kept.

ANGEL SERAPHINA: Eliza's cottage showed signs of being searched after her death. Do you have any idea who did that or what they were looking for?

MONTGOMERY: Wow! No, I have no idea. Was anything taken?

ANGEL SERAPHINA: We're figuring that out. Were you aware Eliza had scheduled a meeting with Angel Force?

MONTGOMERY: No, she never mentioned that. What was the meeting about?

ANGEL SERAPHINA: She didn't specify. Thank you for your time, Miss Montgomery. We may need to speak with you again.

MONTGOMERY: Anything I can do to help, just ask. Eliza deserves justice.

Interviewer's Notes: The subject appeared genuine, although her status as beneficiary provides a motive, but the inheritance doesn't appear to have much monetary value.

Verify the magical security logs for the date in question to confirm the interviewee's whereabouts.

Obtain a full copy of the victim's will to determine the complete inheritance value.

Chapter 22

Roland's whiskers quivered. "It's convenient how Iris's alibi is tied to Zaren's, don't you think?"

I nodded. "And they weren't together the entire night. They finished the stock take around midnight. That leaves a gap."

"Enough time for one of them to have killed Eliza," Sage said. "They both said they were home alone."

"And both have access to magical artifacts and knowledge that could tamper with evidence," I said. "If they wanted something from Eliza's cottage, they'd know how to take it without leaving traces."

Sage's voice hummed through the snow globe. "Iris claims the inheritance is only valuable academically, but magical books are currency in the right circles. *Starlight Bindings* is a rare book. If it's a first edition, it's worth a lot more than Iris admitted."

Roland hissed softly. "And she revealed that Eliza told her about harnessing the well magic. That puts her in the middle of this mess. If Eliza was close to opening a portal at the well, Iris might have wanted in, too."

"Or tried to stop her, and something went wrong." I narrowed my eyes. "Iris also gave Eliza information about binding rituals. She knew what research Eliza was doing, considered it dangerous, yet still helped."

Roland grunted. "Two suspects, neither with great alibis, and both of them dancing around the truth. We need to speak to them. If they're lying, the cracks will show."

"Did Angel Force check Iris's movements on her security log?" Sage asked.

"Not from any of the notes I've read," I said. "But logs can be faked, so it wouldn't prove anything. That's all the suspects Angel Force talked to. Roland, is there anyone they overlooked?"

He shook his head. "No one I can think of."

"What about you?" Sage asked. "I haven't seen your statement."

"They tried to question me." Roland ducked his head. "I was too shocked to say much. When the bond is ripped away like that... well, you know. I could barely remember to eat or breathe. I ended up in recovery three times because my heart almost gave out. I was a mess."

"Did you ever have a prime suspect in mind?" Sage's tone had softened.

"I was too messed up to think straight, let alone solve anything. I thought Angel Force would get it done, but after they wrote up the basics, they stopped caring. I'm no investigator, but I see lousy alibis and obvious suspects right in front of us. It has to be one of them."

"So, we have our suspects," Sage said. "Some with alibis. Some with nothing to show where they were when Eliza died."

"Did you ever hear from Finn about Angel Hogarth, the angel first at the scene?" I asked. "He could have insight into the case."

"Finn said he was strategically retired," Sage replied. "When he checked the HR records, it looked like Angel Hogarth had repeated lapses in judgment. They put him on gardening leave for a year after he complained of night terrors and visions, and then retired him. Finn asked around, but no one knows where he is now. He could be dead."

"Maybe this case was too much for him to handle," I said. "Angels can be so delicate."

"You never say that when Cythera whacks you with a wing for misbehaving." Sage paused. "So, what's the next step?"

"Find the killer and stomp on them," Roland growled.

"That'll happen," Sage said. "But first, you still need three familiars to stop this sacrifice, or you won't be around to find out who silenced Eliza."

"The familiars in this place aren't helpful," I muttered.

Roland's eyes narrowed. "I'll go alone to recruit. This village hates strangers."

"As I've discovered. But who do you trust?"

"There's Whiskers," Roland said after a moment of thought. "He lives in the south quarter. He's young and lost his witch less than a year ago to a creeping fungus. The stuff ate her alive."

Sage made a low, disgusted sound. "Nasty. How well do you know him?"

"Well enough to trust him. He's sensible. He'll help if he can." Roland tilted his head from side to side. "I could ask Midnight. He lives in the cemetery with Morticia."

"Oh, not him," I said. "He jumped me when I wandered around the graveyard."

Roland gave me a pointed look. "What did you expect by poking around the graveyard without an invitation? You're lucky the corpses didn't rise and attack."

"I don't see the issue. Cemeteries are fascinating. All that history etched into the stone."

"And power," Sage said. "Cemeteries hold ripples of the dead's magic. That's what cemetery guardians are for. To keep the magic from being stolen and the dead from rising."

Roland's tail flicked. "There are tabby twins. They live with the retired soothsayer at the edge of the village. They're only young. Less than a year old."

"Will they focus?" Sage asked. "Youngsters are trouble. We had three kittens living here recently. They're part of the reason Juno got exiled. Her past came back and bit her in the butt."

"It was more complicated than that," I muttered.

"It always is with you." Sage's voice grew fainter. "I've got to go. Vorana's back from the store, and I smell treats."

"Save some for me!"

"Are you planning to magic your way home anytime soon?"

I wrinkled my booping snooter. "I would if I could."

"Thought not. Report back when you've got the recruits." The snow inside the globe swirled once more, then settled into stillness.

Roland cracked his neck from side to side. "Let's get to work."

Chapter 23

We arrived at the cemetery just before dusk, Roland in front of me. The light was a peculiar blue-gray that hinted a storm was coming.

The cemetery gates creaked open as we approached.

"That's a bad sign." Roland slowed. "Sacred grounds don't just open for anyone."

"The magic must realize we're here to do good," I murmured.

The gravestones seemed to watch us as we walked along the main path. The whole place vibrated with cemetery magic. Thick, musty, and stifling.

"Something's off," I whispered to Roland. "The magic feels agitated."

"Of course it's off. We're intruding. You stay quiet and let me lead. Midnight!" Roland called out. "We need to speak with you."

The silence that followed was absolute. No insects, no night birds, nothing. Then we heard a soft scraping, like claws on stone. But it wasn't coming from above us. It was coming from below.

The soil at the base of the nearest gravestone shifted and bubbled. A skeletal paw emerged, then another, followed by the grinning skull of what had once been a cat. More graves moved, the earth churning as the feline dead rose.

"Get back. Head for the gates!" Roland hissed, but it was too late. A circle of reanimated cat skeletons surrounded us, their eye sockets glowing with an eerie green light.

"Trespassers," they rasped in unison, their jaws clicking. "Disturbance. Punishment."

I backed against Roland, my fur standing on end. The skeletal cats advanced, moving with jerky, unnatural motions. One lunged for me, its teeth snapping inches from my face. I countered with a deflection spell, but my pathetic magic spluttered into nothing, and it barely slowed the creature.

A bony tail wrapped around my hind leg, yanking me off balance. I felt cold, sharp teeth close around my scruff. The magic emanating from these creatures was ancient and corrupt. Twisted cemetery magic turned against the living.

Just as I thought I was done for, something black blurred through the skeletal horde. Midnight moved like a living shadow, his yellow eyes blazing with fury. With precise, powerful strikes, he shattered the animated skeletons, reducing them to piles of bone.

When the last one fell, he turned the same rage toward us.

"What did you do to anger so many of our dead?" he snarled, his fur standing so straight he looked twice his size. "Do you have any idea what forces you're tampering with?"

Roland stepped forward. "We didn't—"

Midnight wouldn't let him finish. He launched himself at Roland, a missile of fury. They rolled across the cemetery path in a spitting, yowling tangle of fur and claws. I tried to intervene, but Midnight was too fast, breaking away from Roland to slash at my face. I barely dodged in time, feeling the wind of his claws as they passed close to my eye.

"You disturbed the sacred boundary!" Midnight hissed. "Weeks of bone-aching maintenance, ruined. And it'll take me days to reassemble all those skeletons."

"We came to talk," I shouted. "Badger's Haze is in serious trouble. That includes this cemetery. You could lose everything."

That made him pause. Roland seized the opportunity, pinning Midnight with a move I'd never seen before. Part combat hold, part magical binding.

"Listen," Roland growled into Midnight's face. "We're trying to prevent a disaster, not cause one."

Midnight struggled against the hold. "Liars! Only deliberate magical tampering would cause the dead to rise so quickly. They hate you being here. So do I. You need to leave before Morticia finds you. She's not as kind as me when dealing with intruders."

A bone-chilling wind whipped through the cemetery. The temperature plummeted so rapidly that frost formed on the gravestones.

"Too late," Roland whispered.

"Enough!" The word wasn't shouted, yet it echoed with such power that all three of us froze.

A witch stepped from between two mausoleums, and the shadows parted for her. Her silver hair floated around her head, and her eyes glowed with the same green light we'd seen in the skeletal cats.

"Release him," she commanded Roland, who withdrew from Midnight, keeping low to the ground and averting his gaze.

"Bow before Morticia." Midnight sank to his belly.

Morticia glided toward us, each step leaving frost patterns on the ground. Her skin was so pale it was nearly translucent, the veins beneath pulsing with an unnatural green glow. "Would someone explain why my dead felines rose without my command?"

Midnight bowed his head. "Mistress, these interlopers crossed the boundary and triggered the defensive wards."

"We triggered nothing." I kept my voice steady. "The gates opened for us. We were invited inside."

Morticia's eyes narrowed. "Impossible. Unless..." She raised a hand toward me, and I felt her cold magic probing at my aura. "Curious. You bear the mark of exile, yet also the echo of immense power. Where has all that old magic gone? Who was strong enough to take it from you? I would delight in meeting them. They'd be welcome here when it's time to take their final rest."

I didn't reply. What happened with my magic was none of her business.

Morticia turned to Roland, who visibly stiffened under her gaze. "And you, Roland, once bonded to Eliza Thorny. The one who poked at the well until it ate her. Yet you live. A familiar without a witch. Why? What is your purpose?"

"I'm... I'm just Roland," he said quietly. "And we're here about a sacrifice."

The words hung in the air between us. Morticia and Midnight exchanged a long look, that silent witch and familiar communication that left the rest of us feeling excluded. How I missed that.

"The boundary disturbance wasn't from your intrusion," Morticia finally said. "It's been happening for days. I've been watching to see who dares to do this. The people of this wretched place know what happens when they disturb my dead."

"The disturbance must be because of the ritual preparations," I said. "The plan to sacrifice so many people is affecting the balance between life and death."

"Perhaps. We keep out of anyone else's business," Morticia said.

"This business affects you," I said. "Hundreds of people will die. Who will fill your cemetery with power if they're all taken in a sacrifice?"

Morticia lifted her pointed chin. "I shall scoop up the bodies and drain what is left."

"What if this sacrifice leaves you with nothing? Your power will wither like the bodies in the ground."

Midnight hissed softly. "Mistress, if this sacrifice proceeds, the boundary will collapse. With no new bodies to fuel us, we won't have enough power to contain what already rests beneath my paws."

Morticia bared her teeth, her gaze sweeping the graves.

"Does Eliza have a place here?" I asked.

Morticia's head snapped toward me. "What do you know of Eliza Thorny?"

"Only that she was silenced for knowing too much about the approaching sacrifice. And that she was powerful."

"When she came to rest here, you felt the benefit. Her death made you strong," Roland said. "You owe her a debt."

"I owe the dead nothing! They come here so that I may watch them. I sacrifice much to fulfill my duty as a guardian."

There was another silent exchange between witch and familiar. The cemetery grew colder still, frost creeping up my legs.

"One night," Midnight finally said. "I can give you one night to help."

Morticia studied us for what felt like an eternity, her eyes piercing through the layers of my being. I felt exposed, like she could see every mistake I'd ever made, every regret I carried.

"You were cast out for a reason, but perhaps exile has given you a perspective the rest of us lack." She nodded once, sharply. "Midnight will assist you. After that, he returns to his duties. The dead are restless. More than they should be, so we must carefully tend to them. The consequences of not doing so would be worse than this sacrifice you speak of."

I shivered, both from the cold and from the implications of her words.

As we prepared to leave, Midnight called after us. "Don't make me regret helping you, exile."

Chapter 24

After a break to catnap, snack on less-than-tasty treats, and a brief fur groom, we were back on the mean streets of Badger's Haze.

"You'll like Whiskers," Roland assured me. "His witch's death hit him hard, but he bounced back. He's a guru to displaced or abandoned familiars. His advice is always solid."

"That's good to know. We need familiars we can rely on to ensure the anchor points are hit when they need to be," I said.

"We can rely on Whiskers to do the right thing."

The south quarter was eerily quiet, just empty windows staring down at us. We found Whiskers exactly where Roland said he'd be, resting on the stoop of his former witch's potions store, now abandoned and overgrown with ivy.

Whiskers looked adorable, with a fluffy orange coat, white paws, and a white patch shaped like a star on his chest. His eyes were huge and innocent, blinking slowly at us in that way cats do when they want you to think they're friendly.

"Roland!" He bounced up to rub against Roland's side. "It's been forever! And who's your pretty friend?"

I tried not to roll my eyes at the obvious flattery. "Greetings! I'm Juno."

"Ooooooh! The exile?" His eyes widened further. "I've heard stories about you. All the gossip is about Juno, who was trapped here by those mean old angels. Whatever were they thinking? They must have made a terrible mistake."

"It's a long story. But we're not here about that." I nodded at Roland to take the lead.

Roland explained our mission while Whiskers listened attentively. He agreed to help almost immediately, with such enthusiasm that I should have been suspicious.

"Anything for friends, old and new," he chirped. "And I can get us in with a group of outcast familiars. There'll be someone strong enough to help. Follow me. I know a shortcut."

As we followed Whiskers, something felt off. The alley Whiskers led us down grew darker with each step. Where was he taking us?

"Just through here." Whiskers slipped through a crack in a wooden fence. "There's a secret passage. Keep up. You'll soon have your army of helpers. This will be so much fun."

The moment we squeezed through after him, I knew we'd made a terrible mistake. The passage opened onto a small courtyard enclosed by buildings. There were no exits except the way we'd come in, and that entrance slammed shut as three large, mangy alley cats dropped from the rooftops.

"Well done, Whiskers," growled the largest one, a battle-scarred gray tom. "The exile and her friend. We've been waiting to meet you."

Roland whirled on Whiskers. "What is this? We're friends."

Whiskers' innocent facade melted away, replaced by something colder, more calculating. "Sorry, Roland. But the old families are paying handsomely for anyone caught interfering with Badger's Haze business. And it's come to their attention that cases that need to stay shut are being looked into. That's not welcome or wanted."

"You betrayed us for money?" I hissed, backing up as the alley cats advanced.

"For protection," Whiskers corrected. "When you're alone in this village, you do what you must to survive. And for us to survive, you have to be stopped."

The alley cats attacked as one, all teeth and claws. I fought back, but with little magic, the gray tom, his breath hot on my neck, immediately pinned me.

I was all out of ideas, and it seemed luck, that I'd escape this nightmare. But then Roland transformed. One moment, he was cornered, and the next, something awakened in him. The air shimmered, the temperature dropping so rapidly my breath clouded. His eyes blazed electric blue.

"Get down!" Roland snarled at me, his voice layered with power.

I flattened myself against the cold stone as Roland launched himself at the gray tom, not with the desperate lunge of a cornered cat, but with the fluid precision of a predator who'd been waiting for the right moment to strike.

Blue-white energy crackled around his paws, leaving trails like lightning through the air. The tom hissed in shock, swiping at Roland with unsheathed claws, but Roland wasn't there anymore. He'd twisted in mid-air, landing behind his opponent.

"What in the—" the tomcat's confusion was cut short as Roland's murder mittens connected with his flank, sending arcs of magic rippling through the alley cat's body.

The tom convulsed, fur standing on end, before collapsing in a twitching heap.

The other cats backed away, circling warily. One, a mangy brown tabby, feinted left while the other, a scarred black cat, darted right, a coordinated attack that should have trapped Roland between them.

He moved like water flowing around stones and leaped up the wall of the courtyard, rebounding off it with such force that the stone cracked beneath his paws. He became a blur of energy, the magic solidifying into crackling whips that lashed out, catching the brown tabby across the face.

The tabby yowled in pain. He stumbled back, shaking his head in disbelief at the punishing magical blow. "What are you?"

Roland didn't answer. He was already dancing to a rhythm I couldn't hear, moving so fast that sometimes I saw only the afterimages of his magic.

He slid under the black cat's vulnerable belly, leaving a trail of frost in his wake. The black cat's paws stuck to the frozen ground, immobilizing him just long enough for Roland to deliver a series of rapid strikes, each connecting with surgical precision.

The black cat's eyes rolled back, and he collapsed beside his twitching companion.

The tomcat had recovered enough to lunge at Roland from behind. I shouted a warning, but it wasn't necessary. Roland ducked without looking, and the tom sailed over his head, crashing into the wooden fence.

Before the tom could regain his footing, Roland was on him. His paws no longer seemed to touch the ground. They moved in intricate patterns, leaving glowing sigils in the air that burst into blinding light when complete. Each explosion sent waves of magic coursing through the alley cat's body.

The brown tabby made one last desperate attempt, leaping for Roland's throat. Time seemed to slow as Roland pivoted, his body becoming a conduit for magic. He met the tabby mid-air, their bodies colliding in a flash so bright I had to shield my eyes.

When I looked again, the tabby was sprawled motionless beside his companions. Roland stood in the center of the courtyard, magic still dancing around him.

Then it was gone, and it was just Roland, my companion, breathing hard as the magic gradually faded.

The alley cats stirred. As one, they scrambled to their paws and fled through the gap in the fence, leaving tufts of singed fur in their wake.

The courtyard fell silent except for Roland's breathing and the soft crackle of residual magic dissipating into the air. The supernatural chill that had gripped the area gradually subsided.

I stared at Roland, seeing him for the first time. What I'd witnessed defied everything I knew about familiar magic. Without a witch to channel through, no familiar should be capable of such power. Yet Roland had not only channeled magic alone, he'd wielded it with mastery. Did Roland have a hint of demi-god power about him?

"What was that?" I finally managed.

Roland looked down at his paws. "In the cemetery, I felt Eliza stir. It was just a glimmer of what she used to be, but she gave me strength."

I puffed out a breath. "Incredible. Your witch was truly magnificent."

"Almost as magnificent as yours?" He quirked a smile.

I tilted my head. "Almost."

Whiskers cowered in the corner, trembling violently. His eyes were wide with primal fear. "How... how did you do that? Familiars can't channel magic without their witches. Eliza has been dead for years."

Roland walked over and loomed above him. "You're a disgrace. We came to you for help, and you wanted to turn us over to the old families. They're why this place is so broken. They despise change. But if it doesn't happen, we die. Badger's Haze is far from perfect, but it's all we've got. It's our home. It's where some of my happiest memories live. Yours too. Your witch would be so ashamed of you if she still lived."

Whiskers' betrayal turned to remorse as Roland explained again exactly what was at stake, not just for us, but for all of Badger's Haze. The ritual sacrifice would corrupt the natural magic of the area for generations. The village would never be the same.

"I didn't know it was so bad," Whiskers whispered. "I thought you were exaggerating or wanted to mess with the old families. I didn't understand what was happening. I only know that strangers are unwelcome and interference must be reported." He jerked his head at me. "We all hate outsiders. And this one doesn't keep her nose out of other people's business. Juno has been seen poking around. It had to be stopped."

"And now you know what we're really trying to do, does that change anything?" Roland asked. "Or are you still loyal to the families who have done nothing to improve the fortunes of Badger's Haze?"

Whiskers looked up, his eyes clear. "I'll help. For real this time. No tricks. What's being planned, and what happened to Eliza, was wrong. And what I did to you was wrong, too. I'm sorry for tricking you. It'll never happen again."

Roland accepted his apology with more grace than I could muster, and we left Whiskers as he repeated his apologies and promised he'd be ready when we needed him.

Roland was quiet as we made our way back to the library. When I finally asked about his unusual powers again, he simply said, "There's a lot you don't know about me."

That was true of everyone in this cursed place.

Chapter 25

The snow inside the globe spun in a slow, lazy circle before Sage's voice drifted in. "Status report?"

I sat back and let my tail curl neatly around my paws. "We got Whiskers on board. Eventually. But only after he nearly got us killed by turning us over to the old families."

"I thought he was Mr. Friendly. What happened?" Sage's tone was sharp. "Was Juno too sassy for him?"

"I'm always the perfect amount of sass," I said. "The problem is the local old families hate me poking about in their history."

"Who exactly are these old families?" Sage asked.

Roland's ears flicked. "The usual. You get them in all towns. They're the old magical bloodlines. There used to be more of them, but most got out before things turned bad, or they died off. There are still three families here worth keeping an eye on. The Turgletons, who we already know. The Northern Witch Coven, but they keep to themselves now. And the Graphites. They're mean. They don't mingle with us peasants, but they're always watching."

Sage hesitated. "Do you still trust Whiskers after that betrayal?"

"I do." Roland's gaze was steady. "He's easily led and isolated. They must have scared him into working for them."

"I don't," I said. "But I trust Roland's judgment."

Sage let out a sigh. "It's not like you have many other options. You have Midnight and Whiskers, but we still need one more familiar."

Roland's tail tapped against the floor. "There is someone. Another familiar who lost her witch six months ago. But... she's complicated."

I leaned forward. "Complicated how?"

"Her name is Tabitha. She lives in an abandoned greenhouse on the edge of the village. She was bonded to Violet Wildmind."

The name sparked in my mind. "I read about her family in the library archives. Some of the most powerful herbalists this place has ever seen."

"Until recently," Roland said. His voice lost some of its usual sharpness. "Violet died from a strange wasting illness."

"And you know this because...?" Sage prompted.

Roland's eyes slid to the side. "Because I was there. Sometimes."

"Were you a friend of this dying witch?" I asked.

"Not so much her. Tabitha and I had a thing, alright?"

Sage perked up immediately. "A thing? What kind of thing?"

"The kind of thing I do not want to discuss," Roland said, the fur along his spine flattening as if to shut down the conversation.

"Romance," I said in my most innocent voice. "Did it end badly?"

"It must have," Sage said. "You cannot trust Tabitha if you broke her heart."

"I didn't break her heart!"

"Oh! She broke yours. Bad luck." Sage shrugged.

"I'm sorry, Roland," I said. "That's sad. Does she have power, though? Enough to help us?"

"I don't know. She is powerful, but she's not the same since Violet died. She's changed. Tabitha is bitter. Angry. She blames the village for not doing enough to save Violet."

"Can you convince her to help us? Get some of the old Tabitha back?" I asked.

"I can try. But don't expect much. And don't ask about our history."

"Now I'm definitely curious," Sage said.

Roland's eyes narrowed. "Drop it, Sage, or I'll visit Crimson Cove and burn down that dumb bookstore you're always talking about."

"If you find a way out, be sure to bring Juno with you," Sage replied.

Roland hissed at her.

"We'll grab snacks and have a nap, then visit Tabitha," I said.

"Be careful," Sage said. "Cats with broken hearts make dangerous allies."

"I know," Roland whispered. "That worries me. However, she still retains some residual power from Violet. It's exactly what we need."

"It's a risk we have to take," I said. "We're almost out of time."

A shimmer of distortion rippled through the snow globe's glass.

I frowned. "We're losing the connection. Badger's Haze magic is misbehaving again."

"Keep me posted," Sage said. "And Roland?"

"What?"

"Sometimes old flames burn the brightest when reignited."

Roland's tail lashed once. "Shut it, Sage."

The snow swirled again, and her voice faded into the glassy silence, although I was certain I heard her chuckle.

Chapter 26

The moment Roland suggested visiting the greenhouse, his ears had tilted back in that way that meant he'd rather be anywhere else. I didn't push him. Not yet. But I would get to the bottom of his relationship with Tabitha.

We needed a third familiar, and according to Roland, she was the best option.

We left the library and headed back into the gloomy environs of my temporary home.

When we arrived at the greenhouse, it was easy to see that no one cared for this place anymore. The path hadn't been touched in months. Brambles tugged at my fur, and weeds curled up from the cracked flagstones. It smelled of damp earth and old magic, thick enough to taste on the air. It was beautiful in a wild, unkempt way.

Violet's magic lingered here, woven into the soil. If that magic still lived in the earth, there'd be a strong spark in Tabitha. And that gave me hope.

We found her curled on Violet's old workbench, half-buried in dried herbs. She looked smaller than I expected, her black-and-white coat dull in places, the sleek shine worn away by grief and neglect.

When her eyes flicked open and landed on Roland, they widened with recognition.

"Roland?" Her voice was hoarse, like she hadn't spoken in days. "I thought you'd abandoned this place."

"I did for a while," he murmured. "But I needed to be near the last place I saw Eliza alive. And I... visit her. In the cemetery. She's still here, just in a different form."

Tabitha's gaze slid to me, sharp and assessing. "And who's this? A new friend?" There was an edge there, not just curiosity but something darker. I'd expected cool detachment, not jealousy. Did feelings still linger between this pair?

"This is Juno," Roland said. "She's helping me stop a sacrifice ritual. That's why we're here. We need your help."

Tabitha's laugh was low and bitter. "This place deserves to burn. Let them destroy it however they like."

I stepped forward before Roland could answer. "Greetings, Tabitha. We can't allow that. People will die. Innocent people."

"Innocent?" she spat. "No one in Badger's Haze is innocent. They watched Violet die. They had the magic to save her, and they did nothing."

"Violet's illness was beyond magical healing," Roland murmured.

Tabitha's fur bristled. "There were still spell options, but the foolish, idle elders refused to share their books. Cowards. Evil. Let them all die. I will watch and laugh before I join them."

I edged closer and sat in front of her, my paw brushing her side. Her fur was cool under my touch, and I felt the faint, exhausted hum of magic under her skin.

"I understand loss," I said softly. "My witch, Zandra Crypt, is everything to me. She saved me from magic that would have twisted me into something unrecognizable. She taught me how to be kind when it was easier to be cruel."

Tabitha's ears flicked toward me, but her eyes stayed locked on Roland. She didn't speak, and the silence pressed in, heavy and waiting.

"What happened?" she finally asked.

"I was exiled," I said. "Forbidden from ever seeing Zandra again because I misused my ancient magic."

That got her attention. She leaned forward slightly, her whiskers angling toward me.

"I had the power of a demi-goddess," I continued. "I reclaimed it, with a few wobbles along the way. When my home and everyone I loved were at risk, I gave them my magic. It kept them alive and saved them. But Angel Force made a grievous error and believed I caused the danger. They've yet to correct that mistake. They put binding spells on both of us to prevent contact. I can't leave here, and Zandra can't visit."

Roland went still, and I felt the surprise rolling off him. I'd never told him the whole story before.

Tabitha's gaze slid to him. "Eliza came here, you know. She and Violet spent hours whispering together. It was just before she died."

"That's news to me! I went almost everywhere with her. What did they talk about?"

"Violet wouldn't tell me. She said it was safer if I didn't know."

"Help us stop this sacrifice," I said. "If not for the village, then for Violet. And for uncovering the truth about what happened to Eliza."

Tabitha turned away, her gaze drifting to the vines curling over the greenhouse glass. "I have nothing left to live for. My witch is gone. My purpose is gone. I am a shadow. I'll soon be gone, too." She looked back at us, and there was a spark of something in her eyes. "I'll help. Not because I care if this cursed place survives, but because I may as well die doing something other than sleeping among Violet's ghostly memories."

"No one is dying," Roland said.

Tabitha studied him with something close to pity. "You always were the optimist. It's what I—" She stopped herself. "It doesn't matter now. The past remains where it must, and we stagger forward into an unknown future, hoping for better but never receiving it."

Her words were soaked in grief, but her magic told another story. It pulsed faintly in the air, brushing against my fur in cool, steady waves. Power like that would turn the tide in our favor, and maybe lead us to Eliza's killer.

We laid out the details. The ritual. The anchor points. The timing. Tabitha barely needed the explanation since she already understood how magical anchors worked and what it would take to break them. She asked sharp, precise questions, her voice regaining some of the steel I suspected she'd once had.

When we finally left, I walked ahead to the garden gate. My paws crunched over brittle leaves, and I pretended to study a half-collapsed trellis, giving Roland the moment he clearly wanted with Tabitha.

I didn't eavesdrop. Much. But I paused just inside the gate. Behind me, Roland's voice was low and quiet, but I could just make out his words.

"I'm sorry," he said. "For everything. I was in a terrible place after Eliza died, and I didn't want to carry on. During our last fight, I said things I shouldn't."

Tabitha didn't answer right away. "We've made our choices. Now we live with them." Her tone was flat, but not entirely without warmth.

The silence that followed pressed against my fur. I could almost hear the things neither of them said.

Roland shifted his paws. "I'll see you at dusk."

I didn't turn until I heard her call after him. "Roland. For what it's worth, it was good to see you again. And you need to eat more. You're too thin."

We stepped out into the cool night, the air sharp with the scent of overgrown herbs and damp soil. The moon lit the path ahead, pale and uncertain.

We had our three familiars. Midnight, Whiskers, and Tabitha. Each broken in their own way. Each with their own reasons to fight or die.

It was almost time to stop a ritual that had the weight of ancient magic behind it. The odds were against us, but I knew one thing for certain.

We had to try. For Eliza. For the truth.

And maybe, if we survived, for Roland to give Tabitha a reason to live again.

Chapter 27

I should be asleep, since we were getting up early to go over the plan one last time to stop the sacrifice. But sleep refused to find me. My mind raced with plans, contingencies, and the hundreds of things that could go wrong.

If I had my magic, I wouldn't worry. If I had my wonderful witch by my side, I'd brim with confidence. But I was without support.

Well, I had Roland. Could I rely on him and his friends? Did I have a choice? And I had Sage. Although she was never the world's best cheerleader, and could offer little support from so far away.

I'd spent the last hour pacing the library. The ghosts kept me company, but the scholars were unreliable conversationalists, drifting off mid-sentence to debate obscure magical theories with each other. Still, their presence was oddly comforting.

The plan itself was deceptively simple.

At dusk, we took our positions. The sacrifice was scheduled for the moment the sun dipped below the hills. The timing must be perfect. Too early, and we'd alert the perpetrators before our pieces were in place. Too late, and innocent blood would be spilled, powering a corruption that would poison this land for generations and cost hundreds of lives.

Midnight would take the western anchor point, positioned in the old willow grove where the cemetery met the village proper. His task was to disrupt the death magic component of the ritual.

Whiskers would handle the eastern anchor at the edge of the south quarter. He'd neutralize the binding elements that contained the sacrificial energy.

Tabitha would position herself at the southern anchor point, in what remained of Violet's herb garden. Her intimate knowledge of plant magic would allow her to sever the grounding spells.

Roland would tackle the northern anchor point at the tower.

I'd stand guard at the well to ensure no one interfered with its wonky power. As much as it pained me to admit, I was the least powerful magic user in this equation, so I must accept that I couldn't be at the center of this drama.

I'd memorized Eliza's rose poem until I could recite it backward in my sleep. And I knew its value. The first words of each line are action and power words:

Break circle. Scatter light. Call storm. Burn chains. Raise stone. Drown flame.

Those twelve words hinted at what we must do to ensure the ritual failed. If only I had my magic to do any of it.

What also troubled me was what came after. Whoever silenced Eliza must be unmasked. We couldn't allow them to slip away and commit more terrible crimes.

But someone powerful enough to erase such a strong witch from existence wouldn't take kindly to having their plans thwarted. And if they were desperate enough to attempt a sacrifice of this magnitude, what would they try next? And who would they try it on?

Roland slept in the next room, curled up tightly in a nest of old manuscripts. I checked on him an hour ago and found him twitching in his sleep, paws batting at invisible enemies. Even in dreams, he fights.

He was uniquely powerful, and I was glad to have such an ally. Roland wasn't perfect, but after living through such tragedy, he deserved to see justice done.

We were an odd bunch. Midnight, with his cemetery magic and scary witch, who seemed to control him rather than partner him. Whiskers, with his duplicitous heart. Tabitha, with her bitter grief. And Roland, with his impossible powers and heartache.

We were a motley crew of broken misfit familiars trying to save a village that may not deserve to be saved. But save it, we would. Because that's what we did.

"Are you ready? Anything you've forgotten?" Sage's voice floated through the snow globe balanced on the library table.

Roland snorted. "If we'd forgotten something, how would we know?"

I answered for both of us. "We're ready." Mostly. I still had a knot in my stomach, but it wasn't going anywhere.

Roland gave a curt nod. "Midnight, Whiskers, and Tabitha are prepared to move into position when the time's right. I sent messages to all of them. We've got an ethereal communication link set up so we can keep in touch. Juno, you're linked in, too."

"That's not enough," Sage replied. There was a rustle on her end, like she was rifling through spell scrolls. "I'm sending you something. It's a recording spell."

Roland's ears pricked. "A what?"

"Magic transcription," Sage said. "If you fall, at least someone will know what happened."

"Your unwavering belief in us is touching," I said. "You're sending it through the globe?"

"Hold still," she said. "It should connect with you the second it comes through."

The air around me prickled, and Roland muttered, "Huh. Feels tingly. How does it work?"

"It captures everything," Sage explained. "Sound, magical signatures, emotional currents. It'll be a complete record of your actions to give to Angel Force."

"That's genius! Like magical forensics," I said.

Roland gave me a dry look. "More like notes for our headstones."

"The spell will follow you, invisible, recording everything. You need proof of your good deeds," Sage said.

"Will it intervene if we're in danger?" Roland asked.

"No," Sage said. "It observes. It doesn't protect."

"Couldn't you have sent us something with a little more oomph?" I asked.

"This is the best I can do," Sage said. "Anything stronger, and I'll blow up our only way to communicate and get more than a paw slap from Cythera for interfering."

I nodded. "It's appreciated. And I've made myself a collar with pouches."

"It sounds like a dress with pockets," Sage said. "Vorana adores any dress with pockets."

"Similar. The pouches contain magic. I've been working on a few tricks."

"Let's hope you don't need them. May the old magic watch over you," Sage whispered. "Make sure you come back alive."

"We've got a whole day before we're slaughtered," I said. "We might even be back for lunch."

"I can't eat," Roland muttered. "My stomach's twisted."

"Not even a snatch and grab from the butcher?" I suggested.

He hesitated. "Maybe. I don't know."

"Check through the plan again before you set up," Sage said. "And don't get distracted by a tasty sausage."

I shivered, my fur rippling along my spine. "Are you sure this spell you sent us is working? I'm getting chills."

"I forced illegal magic through a malfunctioning globe into a cursed village," Sage said. "It'll take time to adjust. Go walk it off."

"It's not raining," Roland said. "That makes a change. We could walk the anchor points again, see if anyone's left anything there to prepare for the ritual."

I nodded. It was good to keep moving and have a focus, so we left the library and headed toward the eastern anchor point.

A couple walked ahead of us, and I was surprised to see Zaren and Iris. Zaren's steps were slow, and Iris kept turning and gesturing for him to hurry.

"I didn't know they were still friendly," I said to Roland.

He shrugged. "Neither did I. Does it matter?"

I glanced at him. "It does if they're working together to force open these anchor points."

His eyes widened. "We should listen to their conversation."

"Follow me. We'll sneak closer."

"Wait! They'll see you. Your fur is too bright for undercover work." Roland scooped a handful of mud and dirt and smeared it along my sides.

I batted his paws away and hissed. "I was going to suggest you conceal us under a spell. This will take hours to clean!"

He grimaced. "Sorry. No spell, though. Ever since I used my magic to save your sorry behind, all I've wanted to do is sleep. Having no magical tether, it's not so easy to fling out spells and not feel the impact."

I glanced at him. "It really took that much out of you?"

"Yep. I barely use magic anymore. I guess it was my fight-or-flight instinct that kicked in when we were under attack."

"I get it. Let's just be stealthy. No magic. I'm sure we can get close enough to hear."

We hurried nearer, ducking into doorways or alleys to ensure we weren't seen, but Zaren and Iris weren't paying attention, so it was easy to get within earshot.

"...not ready," Iris's voice was faint but distinct.

"You think I care?" Zaren's reply was tight. "We're out of time."

My eyes stayed on them, tracing the bandage on Zaren's hand, the way his other curled into a fist when Iris spoke. "They're nervous. And that kind of nervous usually means danger."

"I can't do this anymore." Zaren's voice floated on the wind. "I'm sick. And I haven't slept in days."

"Pull yourself together," Iris snapped.

"But what if they find out?"

"They won't. By the end of the day, it won't matter. The villagers will have other things to worry about if what Eliza believed comes true."

My ears pricked at Eliza's name. I caught Roland's eye. His jaw tightened.

"I... I keep seeing her face," Zaren said. "She knew something was wrong. I got paranoid that she knew about us. We messed up back then."

Iris's reply came sharp and dismissive. "Eliza didn't care about some pointless fling. She was obsessed with that stupid well and kept on about portals and signs. There were no signs."

"She tried to warn me about the well," Zaren muttered. "I didn't listen. You remember what she was like. One delusion after another."

"Because Eliza was arrogant and thought she could control all magic," Iris said. "Look where that got her. Now she can't warn anyone about anything."

"Were Zaren and Iris seeing each other behind Eliza's back?" I whispered to Roland.

"No way. I'd have known," he said, though he didn't sound convinced.

"I'm more interested in their knowledge about the sacrifice," I said. "They knew Eliza was up to something. Or maybe they were the ones who wanted to access the well power, and Eliza tried to stop them."

"Focus, Zaren," Iris said. "If you mess this up, I'll never forgive you."

"I wanted no one to get hurt. Especially not Eliza. What if she found out and lost focus? She could be dead because of us," he replied.

"If we're doing this, we do it while we still have time. Did you bring the chalk?"

"Yes, and the herbs. But—"

"Concentrate on what needs to be done. This is our one chance to make things right."

"I can't stop thinking about it," Zaren said. "The way Eliza looked at me when she realized what was happening. Like she didn't know me anymore."

"She was too full of pride to think anyone would go against her. That arrogance got her killed. No one is indestructible," Iris said. "She neglected both of us for her precious research. What did she think would happen?"

"What ritual are they planning?" I whispered. "It's too early to force open the anchor points."

"What else can it be?" Roland growled. "I'll run them through with my claws if they murdered Eliza."

"I've considered them both suspects," I said, my gaze still fixed on Zaren and Iris as they hurried toward the market square. "They alibi for each other. Maybe that was a cover, and they've been planning this sacrifice all along. Eliza stopped them all those years ago, but now they're trying again."

"Zaren's just a pretty face," Roland said with a snort. "He couldn't plan a picnic, let alone a mass magical sacrifice. And he doesn't have the magic for it. He's into techy things no one understands."

"Pretty faces make excellent masks," I countered. "And Iris was Eliza's best friend. Who better to know her movements and her secrets? Or to cozy up to Zaren without Eliza suspecting a thing? They could have forged an alliance, killed her, and covered for each other to keep Angel Force from digging too deep."

Roland growled. "How did I miss this?"

"Because they're sneaky. But they're worried the truth will spill out now I've reopened the cold case."

He nodded. "You're right. This must be tied to the sacrifice. I'm not waiting. I'll destroy them."

"No! We need more information and evidence before we act."

"I'm done looking through evidence and hunting clues. I'll force them to confess, then I'll destroy them."

I stepped in front of Roland. "Cool off. I'll watch them and see what they do."

"That's it?"

"No! But killing them won't bring back Eliza."

"It'll make me feel better."

"Really?"

Roland lowered his head. "For about five minutes."

"Exactly. Go inspect your anchor point," I said. "Make sure it hasn't been compromised and we can still access it. I'll keep watching Zaren and Iris."

His tail lashed once in irritation before he turned and skulked away.

Zaren and Iris cut down a narrow side street that led into the square. I hung back far enough to avoid notice but close enough to catch their low, hurried voices.

"It's quiet," Zaren said, glancing over his shoulder.

"It won't stay that way," Iris replied. "We've got maybe ten minutes to do this."

I kept to the shadows of a recessed doorway, my heart thudding. I was about to unmask two killers.

"We lay everything out here." Iris stopped beside the well.

"Don't we need to be closer?" Zaren asked. "Mark the well itself?"

"The water will draw the magic down. That should be enough to make amends."

I cocked my head. Amends? A mass sacrifice of innocents would amend nothing.

"It has to be enough." Iris's tone was taut with something I couldn't read. Fear maybe, or determination. "I'm ready when you are."

"You're sure? Once we start—"

"I said I'm ready. I want this over before we lose our chance. Eliza knew what was coming for Badger's Haze. That's why she died. I'm not dying with any regrets."

Zaren hesitated, his gaze skimming the square. "Let's begin."

I settled in to watch. Whatever they were up to had something to do with Eliza, but I wasn't sure it connected to this evening's planned nightmare.

Iris lifted her head and inhaled.

"Is something wrong?" Zaren asked.

"Just give me a second," she said, and then vanished.

An arm hooked under my front legs and lifted me. My back paws scrabbled uselessly as I twisted, a hiss ripping from my throat.

"I knew we were being watched," Iris whispered in my ear.

I snarled, claws flashing, but she jerked me sideways, and my shoulder slammed against rough brick, knocking the air from my lungs. The world tilted, spinning with the sickening lurch of being lifted off the ground.

I twisted, aiming my murder mittens at her wrist. She jerked her arm back just in time, my claws scraping clothing instead of skin.

"Stop fighting," she hissed. "You're only making it worse."

"Good," I spat. "I intend to make this the worst day of your cheating, murderous life."

Her grip tightened, forcing my head against her chest. I kicked hard, desperate to buy time, but Iris shifted me under her arm like I weighed nothing.

"You should have stayed out of this," she murmured, ducking into a dark passage where the air smelled of damp stone. "Now I'll have to shut you up for good."

"Just confess everything," I yelled. "You'll feel so much better when you do."

"I have nothing to confess. Stop talking." Iris placed a herb-scented hand over my mouth, and the world went black.

Chapter 28

I came back to myself slowly, my head pounding like someone was working out their frustrations with a hammer inside my skull. Cold stone pressed against my side. The air smelled of burned sage and fresh magic.

Before I figured out which way was up, footsteps approached. I shifted, trying to make sense of where I was. My vision adjusted, showing me a cramped room with no windows, just a warped wooden door barred from the outside. The faint hum in the air told me there were wards woven into the lock.

Then memory came flooding back. Iris had discovered me watching. The sudden snap of her hand around me, her magic searing through me, and knocking me out.

I sat up too fast and groaned. My fur felt static-charged, and my limbs ached like I'd run all the way to Crimson Cove. If only I could.

The footsteps stopped, and the door creaked open.

Iris stepped inside and frowned. "I knew my spell hadn't killed you."

I staggered to my paws. "You have no right to hold me prisoner."

She shut the door behind her. "It's your fault. You shouldn't have followed us."

"I wanted to know what you were plotting. What were you doing with Zaren?"

"That's none of your business. Why do you think you ended up here? You poked your nose in where it's not wanted. No one wants you in Badger's Haze."

I took a step toward her. "I know about the affair."

Her breath caught. "What affair?"

"You and Zaren," I said. "I heard everything you two discussed. Is it still going on?"

Iris hesitated, chewing her lip. "Zaren frustrates me. He's so soppy, and he can't move on. Eliza died a long time ago, but he still mentions her."

"So, you are still together?" That was a heck of a motive for wanting Eliza dead.

"No! I ended things straight after her death. I swear."

I kept my eyes on her, searching for the twitch, the flicker that would betray her. "When I first saw you together, I thought you were involved in the sacrifice. You know about that, don't you? You were talking to Zaren about your death being close."

Iris's mouth pressed into a thin line, and she didn't answer right away. The silence stretched between us.

"Maybe," Iris said at last. "What's it to you?"

"I'm stopping it," I shot back. "When I saw you and Zaren heading to the well with ritual items, I figured you were behind the plan to sacrifice so many. But then you spoke of amends. You were planning a redemption ritual?"

Her eyes narrowed. "You know too much."

"That's my mission," I said evenly. "Why attempt such a spell after all this time? As you said, Eliza has been dead for years."

She crossed her arms, her shoulders tightening. "Because of what's about to happen. We wanted Eliza to know how sorry we were. That's all. A spell of remembrance, a cleansing. Nothing dangerous."

"Then why sneak about?"

"Because no one would believe us," she snapped. "Not after the way Eliza died. You've stirred everything up, and we were getting hassled. We came to the well because Eliza loved that place. More than loved it. It was the only thing she cared about. And... if what she believed is true, we're almost out of time to say sorry to her."

I stepped closer, ignoring the ache in my skull. "I can stop what's about to happen. But you need to let me out of here."

"I can't do that. What if you're behind the plan to destroy this place?"

"I'm the only one willing to attempt to stop it," I said.

"You can't! Everyone knows why you were forced to live here," Iris said. "A familiar without magic is just a cat."

"Never underestimate cats!" I glanced past her. "What time is it?"

"Almost dusk. What does it matter?"

"It's almost time for the anchor points to be opened. You must let me go."

Iris growled out a tight laugh. "Give up. No one can stop this. Eliza predicted it, and look what happened to her."

A scuffling sound came from the other side of the door, and it was inched open.

Zaren stepped into view, looking bewildered. "Iris, what are you doing? Why is that cat in here?"

Iris turned. "Go away! This has nothing to do with you."

With Iris distracted, I flew at her, murder mittens at the ready.

"Ouch! Get off of me!" Iris staggered away as I clung to her arm.

"Then let me go!" I twisted hard. "Zaren, where's Roland?"

Zaren's brow furrowed. "Um... who?"

"Eliza's familiar."

"He's dead, isn't he?" Zaren asked.

"This mangy thing will be dead if it doesn't let me go." Iris swung her arm in an arc, making it feel like I was on a Ferris wheel.

"Stop playing with that cat," Zaren said.

"This isn't a game!" Iris yelped as I bit her. "This is the one everyone talks about. The familiar who got herself banished by the angels."

I raked my claws down her forearm, earning another yelp.

"Touch me again," she warned, "and I'll turn you into a hand warmer."

"Zaren." I locked eyes with him. "You're the smart one in this relationship. Translocate us to the well, and I'll explain everything. I can help solve Eliza's murder."

His eyes grew large. "For real?"

"Don't you dare," Iris snapped. "The cat stays here. It's unstable."

"I'm perfectly stable," I shot back. "And you're lucky I don't hex you for eternity for pulling on my scruff. Zaren, we must get back to the well!"

"That's what I keep saying," Zaren said.

"We're going nowhere with this nightmare." Iris finally pried me off her arm.

I bolted for the door, but the wards bounced me back into the room.

Zaren glanced between us. "I don't know what's going on, but we can take the cat with us. I want to finish the spell while we still have time."

"The cat was listening to our conversation!" Iris screeched. "We can't trust her."

"Does it matter?" Zaren asked. "If Eliza predicted correctly, we'll be dead soon. Maybe she can help figure this out."

Iris tutted. "Since you seem so fond of the thing, you take it!"

Zaren tilted his head, one hand hovering in the air. "Why aren't you using any magic to escape?"

"It's complicated," I said. "But I'll use it if I have to. If you want to make amends to Eliza, we must go now. Cast a spell and get us to the well."

He turned to Iris. "What do you think?"

She huffed. "The evil cat is your responsibility."

"I'm all yours," I said to Zaren, "but we have to move."

He hesitated for a second before I allowed him to scoop me up, though every muscle in my body was tense. Zaren grabbed Iris's hand. The air shimmered as he began the translocation spell, the magic vibrating against my whiskers.

The shift hit like a rush of cold water, and the world snapped back into focus as we arrived at the well.

Iris turned to the well, and her eyes widened. "The water is glowing. It's never looked like that before."

Zaren rubbed his temples as if he felt a migraine coming on. "The magic is bubbling up. It feels weird. Does anyone else feel weird? My head is spinning."

"This is bad. I may be too late to help. The anchor points must be opening." I fixed them with a stare. "Zaren. Iris, if you value your lives, you need to run."

Chapter 29

After Zaren and Iris fled, I positioned myself at the well to monitor all points and coordinate through our magical connection.

And although my power was limited, the collar I'd fashioned had small pouches full of magic and charms. I despised collars, but tolerated this one. It could save my life.

I signaled to the others. It was a sad, magical glitter that flicked into the air before fading, but everyone knew the sign to look out for, so they'd be ready to move.

One by one, they confirmed.

"Eastern point secure," Whiskers whispered.

"Southern anchor ready," came Tabitha's steady voice.

"Western boundary a go," Midnight's deep rumble assured me.

Then silence from the north. From Roland. Where was he? I hoped he hadn't seen what happened with Iris and Zaren and was hunting for me. He had to be at his anchor point. If he missed his cue, this whole thing would fall apart.

"Roland, confirm," I pushed the thought toward him. Nothing.

A chanting began, and I tensed as dark figures emerged from the shadows. They wore hoods, so I couldn't see their faces, but their movements were synchronized as if controlled by a power they had to obey.

"Roland?" I tried again, panic rising. "Northern sector, confirm!"

Still nothing.

From my vantage point, I could just make out his anchor. "Whiskers, Tabitha, Midnight, hold your positions. Something's wrong with Roland. I'm going to investigate."

"Hurry," Whiskers urged. "The energy at the anchor point is building. I don't know how long we should wait before sending out the disruptor spells."

"Don't move too soon. If we don't do this together, it won't work," Tabitha reminded us.

I slipped from the well, keeping low to the ground and moving through shadows so the hooded figures wouldn't notice me and try to stop me.

The chanting changed rhythm, growing more urgent, as if it kept up with my rapid paws. Were all the villagers under a haze of broken magic and forced to take part in this ritual? The increasing number of participants suggested that truth.

As I skirted the edge of the largest group, they threw back their hoods, faces upturned to the sky. I recognized some of them from the stores, but their expressions were transformed by fervor, by something ancient and hungry in their eyes.

I shuddered and pressed on toward the northern point. Roland was in trouble, injured perhaps, and unable to respond. He needed my help.

Halfway to his location, I caught movement. A familiar silhouette slipping through the trees, not toward the anchor point, but away from it.

Was that Roland?

Relief flooded me. But why wasn't he at his position? He knew how important this was. Timing was everything in stopping any connection from forming between the anchor points.

I changed course, following him. His movements were purposeful, confident. He must have sensed a problem and was on his way to fix it.

The chanting grew louder, and the ground trembled. If we didn't act soon, we'd be too late.

"Juno?" Midnight's voice in my head was strained. "The energy is peaking. We need to block the anchor points."

"Hold," I whispered, though everything in me screamed to abort, to run. "I've found Roland. Something's wrong."

I crept closer. Roland had stopped in a small clearing. He sat waiting, his tail flicking from side to side. A second later, a figure emerged from the trees. They were tall and cloaked.

"The preparations are complete," the figure said, his voice low but carrying in the air. "The vessels are in position. We await your command."

"You've done well." Roland's voice was different. It was deeper, resonant with authority. "The alignment is perfect. This night has been long in coming."

"What about the investigation?" the figure said hesitantly. "Juno—"

"Is irrelevant," Roland cut in. "A minor distraction. Her efforts will amount to nothing. She's following a lead that will ensure she fails."

My blood froze. Roland wasn't helping, he had caused this nightmare.

"And the others? We watched them gather at the anchors."

Roland laughed. "Playing at parts they don't understand in a production far beyond their puny comprehension. Their attempt at counter-magic will fail without my anchor point being blocked. The balance tips in our favor tonight. We have been stopped before, but never again."

The figure bowed deeply. "As you have foreseen, Master."

Master! The realization hit me like a physical blow. Roland wasn't just involved. He was the mastermind behind it all. How had I been so naïve as not to see this?

Roland had been Eliza's familiar for years. Years of gaining her trust, learning her secrets, and positioning himself at the heart of this magical community. And all for this moment.

I sucked in a breath. Or had something broken along the way? He'd turned to the dark side and believed the only way to get true power was to destroy the person he loved the most.

Roland's head snapped toward my hiding place. "Ah! Interesting. We are observed."

The cloaked figure turned. "Shall I—"

"No," Roland interrupted. "This one is mine. I owe her that courtesy after everything she has done for me."

The figure bowed again and melted back into the trees.

"Come out, Juno," Roland called, his voice almost gentle. "I know you're there. You've always been too curious for your own good, and now look where you find yourself."

I stayed frozen in place, my mind racing. The counter-ritual was failing, and the others were vulnerable, waiting for an opportunity that wouldn't come now that Roland had betrayed us.

Anger bubbled inside me. I'd been so desperate for a friend that I'd grabbed his paw and clung on tight, ignoring any hint he wasn't all he seemed.

"If you're wondering about your new friends," Roland continued, "they're safe. For now. Though I cannot guarantee that'll remain the case if they continue to interfere."

I stepped into the clearing, keeping my distance from him. "Why? Eliza trusted you. She loved you. And you murdered her. Your bonded witch was under your protection. Shame on you."

Something flickered across Roland's face. It was gone too quickly to identify. "Eliza was brilliant. Too brilliant. She suspected me when she found texts that should have remained hidden. Texts I'd been studying. Eliza connected dots that should have stayed separate. She should never have known what I truly was. When she learned the truth, well, I had to act."

"You killed her and destroyed a bond we all hold sacred. That is a disgrace," I spat at him.

"I removed an obstacle." His voice hardened. "As I will remove you. Although I'd prefer not to. You have great potential, Juno. An aptitude for seeing beyond the surface, but not with me. I don't blame you for that. I guided you toward certain conclusions while keeping you blind to others. It was easier than I thought it would be, which is a touch disappointing."

The ritual chanting changed again. Three sharp cries, then silence.

Roland tilted his head, listening. "They're ready for the vessel. Such a shame. You thought you were close to solving this puzzle, and you thought you'd made a friend. All you had were lies and betrayal. How unsatisfactory that your legend doesn't live up to reality."

I ignored the jibe as an icy dread washed through me. "The vessel? You mean the sacrifice?"

"Sacrifice implies waste. This is going to be a transformation. The vessel's energy will fuel something magnificent."

I backed away slowly. "You must be broken since you turned on your witch so easily. It subverts the code familiars live by."

"I am ancient, and I have my own code," he countered. "I've worn many forms, lived many lives. This body, this identity, is temporary. I wear this familiar mask so I can achieve greatness. You should know all about that. After all, you've worn different faces, too."

The chanting resumed, softer now, expectant.

"Who's the vessel?" I demanded. "If you're not choosing a mass sacrifice, then who are you murdering?"

Roland smiled a terrible, knowing smile. "Why, Juno, I thought you'd figured it out. After all, you always act with such certainty. Let me give you a hint. My perfect vessel must be connected to both worlds. The magic and the mundane."

I scowled at him as my mind whirled, then horror kicked me in the gut. "You mean me? That's... that's impossible."

"Is it? A broken familiar with just enough magic to sense the workings, but not enough to take part in them, thanks to the noble sacrifice you brag about. You're perfectly positioned to open a portal to the hidden realms. The ones the old families don't want us to see. Every step you've taken since arriving in Badger's Haze has been guided to prepare you for this moment. Why do you think you chose Eliza's unsolved murder as your first cold case?"

Ice spread through my veins as the truth crashed down. The convenient clues. The way doors opened when they needed to. Roland's unexpected arrival when everyone else in Badger's Haze snubbed me.

"Zaren and Iris are part of your plan?" I needed time to figure out my next move.

"Distractions. Though they played their small part in Eliza's unfortunate demise by sidetracking her from reaching the truth in time. They've served their purpose."

238

A distant chant rose in the night air. It was my name, distorted but unmistakable. They were calling for me.

"They're waiting for you," Roland murmured. "Your destiny awaits. It's time you gave yourself to a greater cause. Isn't that what you do? Such a noble fool."

I ripped open a tiny pouch on my collar and threw a pawful of enchanted iron filings into Roland's face.

He shrieked as the iron burned his magical essence. I didn't wait to see how badly the magic burned him. I ran like fire licked at my tail.

Behind me, Roland's enraged howl cut through the night. "Seize her! The vessel escapes."

I sprinted through the underbrush, my heart hammering against my ribs. The trees blurred around me, branches whipping past my face. I heard my pursuers. Not just Roland, but others, crashing through the woods with inhuman speed.

Perhaps I could reach Whiskers, Tabitha, or Midnight. United, we might stand a chance.

I almost stumbled as a thought thumped into me. Were they in on this, too? I could trust no one. I was alone again. In truth, I'd been alone ever since my banishment to Badger's Haze. The belief left a bitter taste in my mouth.

A figure loomed before me, arms outstretched. I skidded, changing direction mid-stride, and hurled my second prepared weapon, a tiny vial of quicksilver mixed with crushed rowan berries. It shattered against the figure's chest, the mixture hissing on contact. A shriek, then they crumpled.

But there was no time to celebrate. More were coming.

I swerved toward the marshlands, a stinking, sloppy, desolate place no one ventured into. No cat enjoys getting its paws wet, so it might slow Roland.

"Clever, clever Juno." Roland's voice seemed to come from everywhere at once, floating on the night air. "But if there's one thing I learned from the oh-so mighty Eliza, it's that water conducts magic so much better than fire. Why do you think she grew obsessed with the whispers from the well?"

The ground grew sticky. Something grabbed at my hind leg. A tendril of magic, glowing sickly green in the darkness. I hissed and slashed at it with my murder mittens. The tendril recoiled.

"I see you've come prepared with magic you didn't tell me about. Perhaps you're not so trusting after all." Roland's voice sounded closer. "I chose well. You will make the perfect vessel."

"You chose wrong," I spat, fumbling for my next weapon. It was a small stone carrying a charm of deflection. I crushed it between my teeth, feeling the magic spread over me like a second skin.

Just in time. A bolt of energy struck where I'd stood, turning the marsh water to steam. I kept running, the deflection charm absorbing another blast, then another. It wouldn't last long against such power.

The trees thinned. Ahead lay the open ground leading back to the village, and beyond it, the well. I'd come full circle. I couldn't keep running.

Something massive crashed through the trees behind me. I risked a glance back and immediately wished I hadn't. Roland's form had changed, his silhouette against the moonlight was no longer that of a cat but something ancient, twisted, with too many limbs and eyes that burned like coals.

"Enough games," his voice boomed, shaking leaves from branches. "You can't escape your purpose. I will not allow it."

I reached for another weapon. It was a smoke bomb infused with dream essence, designed to confuse and disorient. My paw closed around it just as a wave of force lifted me from the ground and slammed me back down, driving the air from my lungs.

Roland loomed over me, his transformed spider-like shape blocking out the moon. "The chase ends here, vessel. Submit to my will."

I crushed the smoke bomb. Purple-tinged mist exploded outward, filling the clearing. Roland roared in confusion as the dream essence took hold, making reality shimmer and shift around us.

I dragged myself up, every muscle screaming in protest, and limped toward the edge of the smoke cloud, holding my breath so as not to be dragged into the spell's power.

Roland's distorted shape thrashed within it, fighting hallucinations only he saw.

I ran, no longer caring about stealth or strategy, pouring every ounce of energy into survival. Behind me, Roland's enraged howl told me the dream essence was wearing off.

My lungs burned with each breath as I headed toward the place that started it all. The whispering well where Eliza had died.

It loomed ahead, its stone rim ghostly white in the moonlight.

Roland's voice boomed across the square. "Juno! You will be my vessel. There is no other option."

I disagreed. My purpose wasn't to bend to his twisted will. But I had seconds to make a move. No allies. No backup plan. No escape route.

Except one.

The ancient well. Its depth was unknown, with water that had immensely magical properties. Water that was hungry. The water that led to Eliza's death. And maybe, just maybe, where I could be reborn. Or die trying.

I leaped onto the stone rim, balancing for a second. Roland burst from the dissipating smoke cloud, his form rippling between cat and spidery nightmare, his eyes blazing with fury.

He roared, lunging toward me.

And I jumped.

Chapter 30

The darkness swallowed me. Wind rushed past my whiskers as I plummeted, bracing for the shock of the cold water. Eliza's last moments flashed through my mind. Had she considered the same terrible choice?

The impact knocked the air from my lungs. Cold enveloped me, dragging me down. I'd expected to meet whatever had grabbed me the first time I took an unwelcome swim, but I was alone. I sank like a stone.

Above me, Roland's distorted face appeared at the well's mouth, a dark silhouette against the sky. But he was too far away to harm me.

I fought the current with every ounce of strength, my paws slashing through the black water, claws scraping uselessly against the slick stone. The well sucked me down, an ancient throat intent on swallowing me. My lungs screamed, raw and aching, each second a drumbeat closer to drowning.

The water surged again, spinning me in its icy grip. My fur dragged me down like a soaked shroud. I kicked harder, twisting, battering against the current. I would not die. Not in this cursed well.

Even though everything I loved had been cruelly ripped from my claws, I still had a glimmer of hope I'd return to Crimson Cove and my wonderful witch. I couldn't do that if the well magic defeated me.

A weak fizzle of magic clawed through the panic fogging my mind. It flickered, slippery and weak. I hissed through the bubbles escaping my throat, forcing power to rise from my core. The water trembled around me, rippling with threads of energy, but then it faded.

My claws found a crack in the stone. I jammed my paw into it, heaved upward, and slipped. My back legs kicked with wild, furious strength, tail thrashing like a whip. My head broke the surface for a heartbeat, a single, glorious gasp, then I went under again.

The well pulsed with magic, thick and ancient. I shoved against it, my body vibrating with the force of my drained spell as I tried to gain strength.

But I couldn't break free. The well clung to me like a living thing, not just water and stone, but a force with memory, with purpose. My strength faltered, paws slowing. My chest burned. The cold coiled into my bones.

Please...

The word wasn't spoken aloud. I didn't have the breath. But I sent it out anyway, threaded through the tiny remnant of magic humming in my blood. A silent, desperate cry to the well.

Hear me. Please. I know you're not evil. Not twisted. Just abused. Misused by hands that never understood you. But I do. I feel you. I know you. We are as old as each other. Once, I was as powerful as you. With great power comes great trouble. We have both experienced it.

I opened my mind, heart, soul, whatever I had left, and let it spill into the deep.

I am Juno. Familiar to Zandra Crypt. I was something before this body, and I will be something after. I was born to protect. To help. I carry light, even if I don't always remember how to use it. But I want to. Let me live. Let me make this right.

The water shifted. The current reversed, spun and surged with ancient weight. The cold disappeared. My pain vanished, and the burning in my chest dulled, then stopped entirely.

Something touched me. Not claws or current, but magic. Vast, old, and aware. It curled around my limbs, cradling my form like a whisper in a storm.

For one terrible, perfect moment, I felt everything. The well's memory of time, of wishes made and broken, of dark hands stealing its gifts, of laughter, of tears, of power buried beneath lies.

And then it pulled me under.

Not violently, but deliberately. Down, down, deeper still, into darkness so complete. My breath stopped, but I didn't need it. My heart slowed, but I wasn't afraid. I was being drawn somewhere older than death and more alive than the stars.

The magic had heard me. And it had answered.

My paws touched something solid. Not the rocky bottom of a well, but smooth stone. Worked stone. It was a tunnel!

With the last of my energy, I pulled myself into it, finding blessed air. I gasped, coughing out water, trembling with cold.

The tunnel stretched before me, ancient stone swallowed by darkness. Water lapped at my belly fur as I ventured deeper, each step carrying me farther from Roland's rage and closer to... What? Was this a way out of Badger's Haze? I could only hope for such an outcome.

The air changed and became charged, like the atmosphere before lightning strikes, and a familiar scent tickled my booping snooter. Honeysuckle and chalk dust.

"Greetings! I'm Juno. I'm—"

"I know who you are." The tunnel brightened with a soft blue glow emanating from the walls. At its end stood a figure. Translucent, shimmering, but unmistakably Eliza. The Eliza I saw in her shared memory hidden in her home. Not the broken, crystallized body found by the well all those years ago, but Eliza in her prime. She was tall, proud, her robes flowing around her as if caught in an invisible breeze.

"Eliza," I whispered. "You're trapped down here?"

"Bound to these waters by unfinished business and dark magic." Her eyes fixed on mine. "I see you've discovered Roland's true nature."

"Too late," I admitted. "He's been manipulating me all along. The entire investigation—"

"Was his design," she finished. "He needed you prepared, connected, and infused with just enough magic to make you the perfect vessel. I'm sorry he mistreated you, just as he did me."

I slumped against the tunnel wall. "Then I've failed. Everything I did played into his paws. He will finish his plan and destroy so many innocent lives."

Eliza glided closer, casting strange shadows on the tunnel walls. "You jumped down here. Roland would never have foreseen that. That was under your control. Instead of embracing defeat, you tried one more time. That is not failure."

Above us, Roland's voice boomed down the well shaft, distorted by water and stone. "I can sense you down there, Juno. I know you live. The ritual cannot be completed without you, but there are alternatives. I'll take from those you've formed bonds with. Destroy them to punish you."

My blood chilled. Whiskers, Tabitha, Midnight. Were they innocents, after all?

Eliza must have read my thoughts. "Yes, and they're being hunted. Roland's entranced followers have their scent. They won't last for long."

"I must help them!" I turned back toward the well water, but Eliza blocked my path.

"Go up there, and you'll only deliver yourself into his hands. Roland is too powerful to face directly. Especially given your... situation."

I was glad of my fur, so Eliza couldn't see me blush. "I would give up my power again. It was a worthwhile sacrifice."

"I know all about you. I studied you. When I died, I was stuck, so I had time. Your gift of magic was a noble thing. Be proud of that. You helped so many."

"I appreciate those words, but I can't hide while my new friends die, or while Roland finds another vessel and completes his ritual."

Eliza's form swirled, agitated. "Then we fight. Together."

"No offense, Eliza, but you're..." I hesitated.

"Dead?" She laughed, a sound like wind chimes. "Yes. And that gives me advantages."

The tunnel filled with visions, memories playing across the damp walls like moving paintings. Eliza practising spells while Roland watched, his eyes calculating, her discovering ancient texts hidden in the library. And the terrible night when Eliza confronted Roland at the well, and him striking back and taking her life, binding her to the water.

"I discovered his plan too late," her voice narrated over the images. "He'd been working for centuries, taking familiar form, attaching himself to powerful witches, learning their secrets, then moving on when they got too close to the truth and doubted him."

"What is he?" I asked, watching the last scene as Roland transformed into something ancient and terrible with eight limbs and fangs, before pushing Eliza into the well.

"An arachnid being. Something that should have remained buried." The visions vanished. "He seeks to open a gateway between worlds. To let others like him through from realms hidden because they're too unstable and warped."

"Using the sacrifice—"

"Using you," she corrected. "Your unique position between magical and mundane makes you the perfect key."

Roland's voice came again, closer now. He was descending into the well!

"We're out of time." My panic rose. "Can we fuse magic? Work together?"

Eliza's form grew more solid. "It comes with risks. I've gathered power from these waters since my death, waiting for the right magic user to hold them. Before you gave away your energy, you would have handled my magic with ease. Now... it will be a struggle."

"I'll manage. Work through your body."

Her forehead furrowed. "Our energies might not be compatible. You could lose your identity. Or if the possession backfires, I could burn out of existence."

"What other option is there?"

Eliza hesitated. "Even together, we might not be strong enough to stop Roland. He's truly terrible. Darkness has consumed all goodness in him. He must be destroyed. Are you prepared to do that?"

Water rose in the tunnel. Roland was using magic to flush me out!

I backed away from the rising tide. "I'm ready to take the risk if you are. And I'll do whatever I have to stop Roland."

Eliza approached, her form now blindingly bright. "Open yourself. Lower your natural defenses and let me in. I'll do my best not to destroy you."

"And I you." I closed my eyes, relaxing every muscle, every mental barrier. "Why help me? You don't really know me."

"I know your heart." Eliza's voice originated from within my mind. "I've watched you as you found my case and helped. You sought justice for a stranger, and you risked everything to stop a plan you barely understood. You have the soul of a true familiar. Loyal, brave, stubborn to a fault."

The water reached my chest, ice cold.

"Now, Juno. It must be now!" Eliza urged.

I opened myself completely, mentally reaching toward Eliza's presence. For one terrible second, nothing happened. Then, fire filled my veins. I yowl-meowed as Eliza's essence poured into me. Knowledge flooded my consciousness. Spells, incantations, centuries of magical theory compressed into seconds.

My body convulsed, fur standing on end, crackling with energy. I'd always known how powerful Eliza was, but this magic was something else. Even my wonderful witch would struggle to best this tangle of delicious energy.

I've got you. Eliza's voice soothed within my mind. *We're together now. Two aspects of one being.*

The water steamed, and light radiated from my fur, transforming the tunnel into a chamber of brilliant blue radiance.

"Eliza! You are here too. I feel you. I wondered whether your energy had survived." Roland's voice echoed along the tunnel.

We turned. My body, our consciousness, to face him. Roland hung spider-like on the well wall. Multiple limbs, too many eyes, an ancient malevolence given physical form.

"Did you think I wouldn't account for this possibility?" he asked. "A ghost and a failed familiar against a being older than this continent. Don't make me laugh."

He's trying to frighten us, Eliza whispered inside my mind. *Because he's frightened. Roland's grand plan is in tatters. He wants revenge.*

What's he frightened of? I responded silently.

Of what we know.

Suddenly, I understood. Through our merged consciousness, I saw what Eliza had discovered before her death. Roland's weakness.

"You're bound to Badger's Haze," our shared voice called out. "Your gateway portal must open for you to be freed. You made a fatal error when bonding with Eliza. You didn't know that once you entered this place, you could never leave."

This is where the boundaries between realms are the thinnest, Eliza whispered in my head. *Roland needs a way home so he can unite with his allies.*

Roland hissed. "Knowing my constraints doesn't give you the power to stop me. I'm too strong to be defeated."

We raised our paw, my paw, glowing with Eliza's magic, and touched it to the tunnel wall. Ancient symbols carved into the stone centuries ago illuminated one by one. "This isn't just a well. It's a prison."

Roland's form contorted as the magic sprang to life and coiled around him.

"The people who built this village didn't choose the location by accident. They knew this well helped contain terrible things and would keep them safe. Now, it will keep you imprisoned."

Roland launched himself toward us, a nightmare of fangs and blazing magic.

We didn't flinch. Together, we spoke a binding spell, reinforced by our combined power. Well, mostly Eliza's, but I was her perfect vessel to deliver this blast. The symbols on the walls flared brighter.

Roland shrieked, his attack halted mid-leap by invisible forces. "My followers will complete the ritual above ground. They'll sacrifice your friends instead! I'll tell them to do it. You may bind me, but you'll lose your friends, Juno. Friendless and pitiful."

"They'll try." We smiled, feeling our power grow as the ancient binding spell connected. "But those cats are cleverer than you give them credit for. And they're not alone anymore."

With a thought, we sent tendrils of our shared magic shooting upward, through the well water, into the air. Distantly, we felt them connect with Whiskers, Tabitha, and Midnight, conveying warnings and power.

Roland thrashed against his invisible bonds. "What have you done?"

"Given them a fighting chance." Our voice grew stronger as more symbols activated around us. "And ensured you'll threaten no one again."

We pressed our advantage, moving closer to Roland's struggling form. The water rose with us, but now it responded to our will, curling around Roland like liquid chains.

He snarled, his multiple eyes blazing with hatred. "I've waited centuries for this moment. I can wait centuries more."

"But you'll wait alone," we replied. "No more victims. No more vessels. And this well will be sealed for good."

There was one weapon left on my collar. Eliza's vial of blood, willingly given and brimming with power. I unhooked it and tossed it at Roland.

With a final, terrible shriek, Roland's form collapsed in upon itself, drawn back toward the deepest part of the well, down to whatever ancient chamber would be his eternal prison.

As he vanished into the depths, he tossed out a blaze of power. Stone cracked. Magic shrieked, and we were hurled from the well, a glowing streak of light and smoke.

Chapter 31

We landed in the square, claws scraping cobblestones, paws skidding. My fur sparked with magic, threads of green and silver rippling through my coat. Eliza hummed just beneath my skin, steady, guiding.

Around us was chaos.

Shadows surged. People moved like marionettes, their eyes blank, and limbs stiff. Possessed. Controlled by Roland's power, even though we'd trapped him. Badger's Haze was burning under a magical collapse.

In the center of the chaos, my new friends fought.

Whiskers launched himself from a roof onto the back of a possessed villager, sinking his teeth into the man's shoulder and sending a wave of golden light through him. The man dropped, the spell broken.

Midnight, sleek and quick, darted through legs and shadows, scattering powder from a pouch around his neck. Wherever it landed, followers howled and staggered, blinded and confused.

Tabitha stood alone, a whirl of claws and chants. She hissed and slashed at anyone who came near her.

"We must deactivate the anchor points," Eliza said from inside me. "The possession is spreading. Even though we've trapped Roland, he'll have an army of mindless servants at his command. They'll destroy Badger's Haze."

A blast of magic came from our left. I didn't dodge. I leaped into it. The spell struck me, and we bent it before flinging it back in a glowing arc that slammed into three villagers. They fell with a collective moan, smoke rising from their chests.

We glided low and fast, weaving between limbs and flares of light, slicing through the chaos. My murder mittens sparked with energy, each swipe undoing dark enchantments. Eliza channeled spells through my body like I was a living wand.

We reached Midnight first. Two bulky villagers wielding crude charms made of bone and blood had him cornered.

I hissed once. The air split, and a wave of silver-green light burst from my chest, knocking the men back like leaves in a gale.

Midnight gave me a flick of his tail in thanks and vanished into the fight.

We turned and sprinted toward an unguarded anchor. It pulsed with unstable energy, a possessed woman scrawling over it in glowing ink.

I leaped, claws out, and struck her chest. She screamed, spun, and Eliza spoke a word through me in an old, forgotten tongue.

The anchor flared, and the woman froze mid-movement, then crumpled as the possession spell left her.

A tremor ran through the ground.

Eliza stirred inside me. *An anchor awakens. It will still do damage if it activates. Summon your friends. We need more magic to silence it.*

We ran. Tabitha, Whiskers, and Midnight followed as soon as they heard the call for help.

Thick fog smothered the northern edge of Badger's Haze. As we neared, the trees warped and shimmered like mirages. Magic throbbed through the earth, erratic and unstable.

The ground glowed as a pale, wild-eyed young woman hovered over the anchor point, her arms outstretched, mouth moving in some ancient, twisted chant.

She turned toward us, her eyes completely white. Then she screamed, and magic cracked like thunder.

A wave of shadow rushed at us, and we scattered before it made contact. I darted left, barely avoiding a lashing whip of black light. Tabitha tumbled and rolled. Whiskers and Midnight flanked from the right.

"She's draining the anchor," Eliza warned me. "If she finishes, it'll collapse. We must break the circle she's forcing into existence."

"Just as your rose poem told us to do." I launched forward, my paws skimming across the grass, claws glowing with Eliza's energy.

Spells lashed out from the floating woman to stop us. Crimson bolts, spikes of ice, tongues of green flame.

I dodged, twisted, felt one graze my flank, but kept going. Midnight flung a vial of shimmer-dust that exploded midair, blinding the woman long enough for Whiskers to charge beneath her.

But the woman caught him mid-pounce with a flick of her wrist, and he was thrown back into a tree with a sickening crunch.

"Whiskers!" I shouted.

"I'm fine." A groan followed those words. "Keep going."

I focused, channeling Eliza's strength, and drew power from the anchor itself, calling on the old magic. The air thickened, and energy coiled through my limbs like liquid fire. The anchor point wanted our help. It didn't want to be destroyed or destroy.

Together, Eliza and I spoke the words from her poem. *Break the circle. Scatter the light. Call a storm. Burn the chains. Raise stone. Drown the flame.*

A pulse of pure light cracked across the ground and knocked every leaf from the trees.

The woman shrieked, flailed, and flew backward.

The anchor stone flared white as a storm gathered overhead, lightning so sharp it almost blinded us. A single shaft of lightning smashed into the anchor. Magic raced from it to the other anchors, completing a circuit.

A sickening sensation slithered through me. Had we failed?

Wait, Eliza whispered in my mind.

"But they're connected," I said. "We didn't make it in time."

Just wait. You'll see. The chains are being burned.

I dropped to the ground, panting, fur smoking slightly, paws trembling, still uncertain we'd succeeded.

Tabitha came to my side, limping. "Did we do it?"

Whiskers dragged himself over, one eye swollen. "I hope so. I lost a tooth." He flopped down.

Midnight perched nearby, scanning the trees. "I don't see any looming apocalypse, although I have no clue what that would look like. I'd expect there to be wailing. Probably zombies. Maybe a few ghouls. The usual dark chaos."

Inside me, Eliza exhaled. *The anchors connected to good, not evil. Watch.*

A flare of pure white light surrounded the boundary edge, sweeping across every building and yard and swiping away the dregs of Roland's darkness.

The fear slid from me as I realized the truth. Badger's Haze was safe.

We staggered back to the well. My new friends limped beside me, fur singed, whiskers bent, eyes weary.

The people still standing were shaking their heads, confusion on their faces as they figured out what they'd stumbled into. Would they ever know how close they'd come to dying?

The well shimmered faintly, but the magic was calm. There were no whispers beckoning us into its curious depths and no signs of any nightmare spider ancients wanting to drag us to our doom.

"Let's finish this and raise the stone." My voice was rough from smoke and spell work. I still felt Eliza inside me, solid, present, our bond humming beneath my skin. It differed from the bond I had with Zandra. Could Zandra feel this? Would she wonder who I'd connected to? Would she worry about our bond breaking?

"We must seal the well," Tabitha murmured, hobbling forward.

I stepped up and peered into the depths. The water was smooth as glass.

Wait, Eliza whispered in my mind. *Something's wrong. How? I still feel him. He shouldn't be able to get free.*

A hand. Clawed, burned, twisted with veins of green-black magic shot from the well like a viper.

Tabitha yelped and stumbled back. Midnight hissed. Whiskers' hackles lifted.

And Roland emerged. The thing that pulled itself from the well was corrupted, bloated with dark power. His eyes bled light. His skin was cracked marble etched with runes.

He grinned, and his teeth were too sharp. "You thought your magic would hold me? You thought you could undo everything I'd put into place? So arrogant. So stupid."

I stepped in front of the others, my murder mittens flexing. "We knew we could stop your sacrifice. You lost."

Roland's laugh sounded wet and wrong. "You've sealed the anchors. Clever cat. But you forgot one thing..." He raised a hand. The sky fractured, and the well glowed. "You can't stop broken magic when it's hungry. And this well is always hungry."

The ground opened, cracking beneath our paws and trying to swallow us.

"You should have stayed in the well." I felt no fear in confronting Roland. Not with Eliza and my friends by my side.

Roland thrust his clawed hands forward, and black fire screamed toward us.

I jumped. Mid-air, Eliza cast a ward so old it echoed in my bones. Roland's fire hit it and shattered like glass.

I landed on Roland's chest with a snarl, my claws sinking in. He howled, staggered back, and with Eliza's power surging through me, I bit into his withered, ruined soul. He screamed as the toxic magic unraveled inside him.

"You misused the well," Eliza said, her voice woven into the air. "You misused *me*. That ends now. I loved you, Roland, but all you cared about was power. Your cold cruelty will never win."

Roland flung one last burst of wild power. It cracked through the sky and struck the library, scattering out lumps of stone. But he was weak, and this was a final desperate act to cling to the power he'd come so close to controlling.

We pinned Roland, murder mittens and magic stopping him from rising.

"Let the people of Badger's Haze go free," I hissed into his face. "They deserve better than to be your slaves."

"Why save them? You loathe this place. You've complained every day since your banishment. Don't pretend to care."

My claws pressed harder into his shoulder, but it was Eliza who moved us closer.

"You were *my* familiar," she whispered. "I chose you. I trusted you."

"You used me," he snapped, writhing. "You fed me scraps of power while I sat at your feet like a servant!"

"I gave you everything I could." Her voice cracked like thunder. "You betrayed our bond."

"You have no power over me now," he spat.

Eliza raised my paws, causing them to shimmer with pale gold light, shaky but gathering strength. "You forgot the most important thing when you bonded with me."

"And what is that, you foolish witch?"

"You never released the oath. That single oath and bond that cements a familiar to their magic user."

Roland stilled. Magic drew close, ancient and cold.

I hissed, knowing what was coming and longing to back away from the crackling tension, but joined magic trapped me. "Eliza. There must be another way."

A trickle of sadness shifted inside me as Eliza's mixed emotions swirled to life. "I wish there was, but we have seen what he can do. I must prevent him from hurting anyone else. I'm sorry you must witness this, Juno, but it's the only way to guarantee Roland will hurt no one ever again."

My throat tightened, not wanting the words to escape, but Eliza forced her power through me as she lifted my paws higher. "By the pact made and broken, by the bond betrayed, by the name shared in trust, I call the familiar oath home."

"No!" Roland thrashed.

Eliza's magic flared, a circle of white fire surrounding him. "Let what was stolen return to the earth, let what was twisted unravel, and let the traitor be cast out!"

The light surged. Roland screamed, not from pain but from loss. The power he'd siphoned from Eliza and used to control Badger's Haze was ripped out of him along with the enduring bond forged by a witch and their familiar.

I'd done it myself, and still bore the scars. I felt it like claws on bone. The bond being undone tore at something old and sacred in me.

The fire died. Roland collapsed, shivering and diminished. He looked up, hate burning in his eyes. "You think this ends me?"

"No. This does." Eliza turned us toward the village well. She muttered a second spell, and the air bent inward, folding around the shape of the well like glass forming over flame.

"We bind you here by raising a stone barrier," she said. "To the place you took. You'll guard it now, silent and unseen. Forever. There will be no more sacrifices. You'll satisfy the well for eternity."

The light swallowed Roland. His scream echoed, then vanished as he plummeted into the depths one final time. The well settled, and a trickle of sparkles shivered into the air as a wall of stone encased it.

And just like that, Badger's Haze was truly free.

Eliza was quiet in my mind, but I felt her smile.

"We did it," I whispered, licking my paw clean of some gross goop.

The fight was over. Eliza's murder was solved, and a quiet resolve and acceptance returned to my temporary new home.

Chapter 32

I'd updated Sage the moment I got back last night. She was still in shock when I contacted her again this morning, pacing the living room, her harness clattering, as she kept going over everything that happened.

"So, Roland was evil." She finally settled, her nose pressed close to the glass.

"Yep. And I didn't see it until it was almost too late," I said.

Her gaze softened. "That's sad. You liked him."

"I trusted him," I said quietly. "That's different."

She glanced away, as if the thought pained her too. "But Badger's Haze is still standing. You won."

"For now." My paw went to my chest. "Eliza's still here."

Eliza's voice echoed in my mind, warm and gentle but tinged with sadness. *Our bond is unraveling. I must let you go. My power will cause you harm if I stay any longer.*

"You need to go now?" I asked. "I kind of like having you around."

I must thank you. After all those years trapped and forgotten, I was remembered. I mattered again.

"You always mattered," I said. "Badger's Haze will never forget you. I'll make sure of it. Maybe a memorial herb garden in your name. Do you approve of that idea?"

I'd like that. Thank you for being brave enough to let me in. You saved them. You saved me.

"You saved me, too."

Live well, Juno. Although maybe stop jumping down cursed wells, hmm?

"No promises." I was quiet for a second. "When we separate, what happens to you?"

My time ended when Roland trapped my spirit in the well. You freed me, so I can rest in peace. Tell Roland—the real Roland, my true familiar—that I loved him and I'm sorry I couldn't protect him.

I frowned. "The real Roland? Didn't we defeat the real Roland?"

Not all is as it seems.

"What does that mean?"

Her presence slipped away like water through my paws. A strong smell of chalk and honeysuckle lingered before fading.

"Eliza?" I called into the silence of my mind. "Who is the true Roland?"

No answer.

"She's gone?" Sage asked.

"I guess so." My voice came out rougher than I'd intended.

"Are you okay with her leaving?"

"Not really. But I will be." I rubbed my forehead. "She said something weird, though. She said there's a real Roland."

Sage's brow furrowed. "I don't understand. Roland was the villain."

"Eliza sounded like she wasn't talking about that Roland," I murmured. "I need time to process."

"Are you okay?" she asked again.

"You've already asked me that."

Sage leaned closer to the globe. "Look in a mirror."

I did and froze. My fur was faintly luminous, a soft glow pulsing under my skin like moonlight caught in water. "Oh, wow. My paws are tingling. Do you think I kept some of Eliza's power?"

Sage tilted her head. "Maybe it was a gift. Eliza gave you magic so you could find the other Roland. Perhaps the real Roland was her familiar, and the entity you fought was a copy of his form. It wouldn't be the first time something like this happened."

I flexed my paws, feeling a strange hum of energy ripple through me. "Some dark magic users keep a living vessel alive so they can take its shape. This feels like a new mystery waiting to be solved."

"Or," Sage said with a faint smile, "it's the same mystery with one more piece to find. And you're going to hunt for it, aren't you?"

"I always do."

She raised her chin. "Not today, though. Today, you rest and heal."

I thought about arguing, but the ache in my limbs won. "Fine. A nap, a bath, and some snacks. Then I look for the real Roland."

After an epic catnap that lasted most of the day, I went looking for Roland. The *real* one. Not the twisted, snarling spell-corpse we'd fought and flung into the well, but the incredible cat Eliza had loved.

A surprisingly fresh breeze laced with prickles of ice bathed Badger's Haze. The dampness made my fur fluff. You could always guarantee the weather would be lousy in this place.

I started my search for clues at Eliza's cottage. I stopped at the entrance. Someone had left a note tucked into the doorframe.

Thank you for protecting us.

No name. Just that.

Inside, the cottage was empty. I nosed through the bookshelves. Nothing about Roland. No photographs or paw prints.

After finding nothing useful in the cottage to suggest where Eliza's true familiar could be, I stood outside and breathed in deep before heading into the unhelpful center of Badger's Haze.

I tensed when a man rushed toward me. He flung down a slice of honeyed salmon on a step and ran.

A moment later, a girl with ribboned braids offered me a tiny bouquet made of feathers and dandelions. She didn't speak, just looked at me like I was something out of a bedtime story, then hurried away.

This was different. The villagers no longer saw me as trouble, but as someone who fought beside them. Bled for them. Saved them. It felt good not to be despised.

After I'd walked the edge of the village and circled the anchor points, I paused beneath an old ash tree close to the newly enclosed well.

No whispering voices were encouraging the clueless closer. There was just the soft sigh of magic at rest. But still no clues as to where the missing Roland may be.

I left the sealed well and ventured deeper into the village, hoping someone might have seen Roland before his evil magical doppelganger took over.

My first stop was Mrs. Kettleworth's café. It was a dingy place with bunting long overdue a wash, but she was fond of cats and often left out saucers of cream for strays. She'd remember the real Roland.

I approached her as she arranged scones on a tray. When she spotted me, her hands paused over the treats.

"Oh," she said, her voice carefully neutral. "It's you."

I sat politely. "Greetings, Mrs. Kettleworth. I'm looking for Roland, Eliza's old familiar."

She turned back to her scones. "He vanished at the same time as Eliza. Though I wondered... no, it's probably nothing. My old eyes play tricks on me."

"What did you wonder? Did you see him? Please, anything might be useful. I think he's in trouble, and I want to help him."

"Out you go. I can't afford to be seen with the likes of you. You've done a good thing, but we all know the reason you're here. I won't lose customers." And with a flap of her towel, I was shown the door.

I tried the fishmonger, the baker, even the woman who sold used books. Each conversation followed the same pattern. There was an awkward acknowledgment of my help, hurried thanks, then a swift dismissal. They were grateful, but gratitude mixed with fear created an uncomfortable distance and no answers.

It was old Mrs. Brambleby who finally gave me something useful. She was tending her vegetable patch when I found her. She wore a hat that was once a tea cozy and was the kind of ancient witch who probably knew Merlin and had told him to wash behind his ears.

"Greetings, Mrs. Brambleby," I said. "I'm searching for Roland, Eliza's old familiar."

"That Roland," she said without looking up. "He always was a wanderer. I used to see him up near the cemetery. He liked to hunt mice and take them to Eliza. She'd scream blue murder when she found one resting on her shoe as a gift."

"We only leave those gifts to show you how much we care."

She straightened with a grunt, wiping soil from her hands. When she finally looked at me, she froze. "It's you! I didn't realize who I was talking to. I should go inside."

"Please don't leave. I need to find my friend. He's in trouble."

Mrs. Brambleby gathered her gardening tools. "Roland is gone. And you should be, too."

"Wait! If you were to look for him, where would you go?"

"A coffin!" Without looking back, she hurried inside her shed and shut the door.

It was a risk, but I needed to explore the cemetery. The clue provided by Mrs. Brambleby was all I had about where Roland spent his time before the many-legged spider monster copied his form.

After a careful check to ensure Morticia and Midnight weren't stalking among the headstones, I slid under a gap in the fence. Damp earth and dried roses scented the air. Even the wind was quieter, as though trying not to disturb the dead.

Despite the creepy vibes, it was beautiful in a gothic, unsettling way. Twisting iron fences curled like vines around old mausoleums. Ravens watched from crooked trees, their glossy feathers ruffling. Moss-covered angels leaned, their wings cracked with age.

If the real Roland were alive, someone might have trapped him in a part of the cemetery few people visited. Somewhere shadowed and neglected.

After some searching, I discovered the western edge of the cemetery appeared rarely used, its graves sunken and abandoned. Weaker magical families must have buried their dead here, and they needed less monitoring.

I slipped through an arch of crumbling wood and ivy and paused. There was a patch of earth darker than the rest. I moved closer, every step hesitant. There was no headstone. No flowers. Just unsettled soil and the faintest shimmer of residual magic hovering above it.

There was a rustle in the hedgerow, and I whipped around, fur puffing out. From the mist beyond the nearest crypt, Morticia stepped into view. Layers of fabric draped her body, unmoved by the breeze. Her hair was white as candle wax, and her eyes glowed faintly blue.

I backed up, one paw landing in the freshly turned earth. She hadn't seen me, but it wouldn't be long before she sensed my presence. Maybe she already had, and that was why she was on patrol.

Morticia raised a single long finger and held it up as if testing the air. Her tongue flicked out, and she frowned. "I know you're here. You cannot hide."

The ground shivered, and a low groan came from beneath the earth, like something ancient shifting in its sleep.

I bolted, claws scrabbling over stone, dodging around angel statues and mausoleums, my heart hammering. Behind me, the wind howled through the trees, and something growled. It could have been Midnight, but I didn't stop to check.

After making it to the gate, I launched myself through the bars just as they snapped shut behind me with a clang like a death knell. Breathing hard, I didn't stop until I was halfway down the lane and heading back to the library.

That was too close a call. With little magic to protect me from Morticia's vigilant guard, I'd never figure out if Roland was in the cemetery.

But I'd keep searching until I found him. I just needed to find another way.

Chapter 33

I was crouched over the circle I'd drawn on the floor, whiskers twitching with concentration. The magic sparked. It was a sharp jolt that snapped through my paw and made me hiss.

"You're doing it wrong. Again," Sage muttered.

"I'm doing it differently," I shot back. "There's a subtle distinction."

"Subtly ineffective," she said.

I fought the urge to swipe the spell diagram into a smudge. "It's new magic. It's allowed to be temperamental. Ugh, I just shocked myself again. Using someone else's power is never easy, but I'll get used to it. I need this location spell to find Roland."

Sage frowned. "I can't get a clear fix on him from here. I keep pulling up something, but it's hazy. Without a personal item or a drop of his blood, I can't lock on properly. Maybe you need to accept he's dead and we're picking up his residual magic. Few familiars survive long without their witches. It's unnatural. We should have realized something was off when Roland showed up in your library.

You don't live for twenty years without your bonded witch."

"Everything about Eliza and Roland's bond was rare," I said. "Much like mine is with Zandra. He's alive. I know it."

"You can't be sure of that. What do you see when you cast the spell?"

"Blank spots across the village," I admitted. "But I keep getting a strange black dot hovering over the cemetery. Every time I touch it, my paw aches."

Sage's eyes narrowed. "That could be Morticia's magic messing with you. That cemetery guardian hates you. And she knew it was you who snuck in earlier."

"You're right. I think she cursed me. Ever since I fled the graves, my paws have been filthy. I clean them, turn around, and boom, dirt all over them again. Not normal dirt, either. It smells old, like I've snuggled with a desiccated mummy."

"Are you sure it isn't from your failed attempts at using Eliza's magic?"

"This feels different," I said. "The dirt is crumbly, gray, and cold. It sticks to me like it has a grudge. Sometimes it glows faintly blue."

Sage sat forward. "Describe it again."

"Crumbly, gray, cold. Gritty. It smells like dried roses and damp stone."

Her eyes widened. "That's grave dust!"

"Wonderful. How do I get rid of it?"

"You don't," she said. "Not until you've figured out who sent it to you."

"It wasn't Morticia?"

"She'd want to keep you out. That grave dust is an enchanted invitation."

I tensed and peered at my filthy fur. "Could it have been Roland?"

Sage's face lit with excitement. "Yes! Grave dust is a basic element. If he's trapped, he might be too weak to do anything else. He could be sending out faint pings of magic through the dirt. That dot you keep seeing isn't Morticia's power. It's Roland's! He's trying to break through. You were right. He's in the cemetery."

"I stepped in some freshly turned earth when Morticia scared me. We could have connected through that." My chest tightened. "All this time. Over twenty years of being trapped underground. How... how will he be?"

"Not good. But he's still holding on," Sage whispered. "That cat has serious power."

"Having sensed Eliza's magic, I know the real Roland will be incredible," I said. "I'm going back to the cemetery."

"You'll never make it past Morticia. She'll destroy you."

A sharp bang cracked from outside, rattling the windows.

Sage jumped. "What was that?"

I flattened my ears, listening hard. "Hopefully not Morticia."

"Ignore them. It's probably someone selling dodgy grimoires."

The thudding continued.

"It could be important," I said.

"Staying alive is more important than investigating that noise."

The library doors shuddered, then burst open with a bang loud enough to topple a pile of dusty books from the nearest shelf. A moment later, Midnight barreled in, his fur bristling, eyes glowing.

I hurried toward him. "If this is about me being in the cemetery—"

"It's not. Although I'll have words with you about that later," Midnight said. "We all got messages."

Tabitha swept in behind him. "Not messages. Dreams. Roland came to us."

Whiskers waddled in last, a packet of dried sardines clamped proudly in his mouth. He dropped it at my paws with a thud. "For the road. You can't fight the undead on an empty stomach."

"Roland contacted all of us?" I asked.

"Yup. What did you get?" Midnight asked.

I glanced at my filthy paws. "Persistent grave dirt."

Midnight smirked. "Nice. He tried to speak to me in a dream, but he had no voice. His eyes glowed, and the dirt clung to his fur. And then the earth cracked open beneath him."

Tabitha set something gently on the floor. It was an old collar, damp with clotted earth. The metal tag hummed with a faint blue light.

"Where did you get that?" I asked.

"At the entrance to my greenhouse this morning," she said softly. "It wasn't there last night."

I stretched out a paw, and the magic pulsing through the collar thrummed against the lingering dust on my pads. It was the same signature. Same desperation. Roland.

"I know where he is. He's buried in the cemetery," I said.

Midnight squared his shoulders. "Then let's go. I'll handle Morticia. The rest of you find Roland and dig him out."

We headed out of the library and slipped into the cemetery, more confident with Midnight as our protector.

I led them to the area that kept revealing a black dot on my location spell and brushed off some of the crumbly grave dirt that coated my fur. "You want to be found, don't you, Roland? Show us where you are."

I tuned into my new magic. Elemental magic was a slippery mistress, and I struggled to control it, but I gripped it tight as I recited a spell. "Let the lost be found. Let the bound be free. Show me where he waits." My paw sparked. The dirt lifted, floating mid-air like ash. A thread of gold light flickered from it and zipped away.

"Oh!" Tabitha gasped. "I didn't think you had much magic."

"It was a gift from Eliza. If anyone's magic can find Roland, it's hers. Let's go!"

We followed the glowing thread, darting between cracked tombstones and gnarled trees. The light twitched like a nervous tail, winding around broken statues and down a slope, taking us into the abandoned section of the cemetery.

The thread led us to the rectangle of disturbed earth. Something vibrated beneath our paws.

276

"It's him!" Tabitha shook as she stared at the ground. "My Roland is trapped here. Help me get him free." She dove at the dirt.

We all dug. No fancy spells, just clawed like wild things, tossing clumps of wet earth and broken roots.

Whiskers yowled, "I've got something!" He revealed a small tin box the size of a bread bin.

I crouched beside it, anticipation fluttering in my stomach. "Roland? Are you in there?"

There was no reply.

Midnight leaned closer. "Maybe he's—"

The box moved. Just a twitch. A scrape. Like claws against the inside. Then a voice, hoarse and fragile. "Tabitha?"

We tore the lid free. Inside was a gray, bony, barely breathing cat. His fur was matted and thinned, his eyes dim but still lit with weary warmth.

"Roland," I whispered, but I was shoved aside and landed in the hole as Tabitha barged past to reach him.

Midnight scowled, his top lip curled as he tasted the air. "This is some nasty dark magic. Old magic. It's making me sick to my stomach just being close to it."

Roland whimpered and tried to sit, but failed.

"Don't struggle. We'll get you out," I said. "And we're getting you home."

He blinked. "I don't have a home, do I? Eliza is dead. I felt her go. For good this time. She's always been here, lingering in the breeze, looking for me, but we could never connect. Not with the magic wrapped around me. Then something changed. I felt it. Eliza went, and I felt... free, but I couldn't move. I didn't want to."

My throat clenched, and I pressed my head to his. I felt threads of icky magic wrapped around him, tight like chains. He hadn't just been buried. Roland was anchored to this place.

"We're setting you free. No one deserves this," Tabitha said, her voice hoarse with emotion.

Midnight and Whiskers stood guard while Tabitha pawed gently at Roland's side, careful not to jostle the magic threads and hurt him. They hummed beneath him like twisted vines, pulsing faintly with something ancient and wrong.

Roland's eyes found mine. Foggy, dim, but finally clearing. "Eliza..." he breathed, then shook his head. "No, not Eliza. But she's close. So close. Are you... how do you know her? You smell like her."

"Greetings, I'm Juno," I said. "Eliza gifted me a small piece of her magic. It stayed with me when she crossed over. Thanks to her, she made sure you wouldn't be stuck here forever."

His eyes widened, and a shimmer of cleverness flickered there. "That's how I felt her! Through you. A familiar carrying a witch's magic when they aren't bonded... it's unheard of. But Eliza always broke the rules."

"I'd have gotten you out," Tabitha whispered. "But none of us knew you were still here."

"I didn't know where I was either," he said. "Not really. Not for a long time. The thing that took my place trapped me in a spell, then buried me, and used my shape. I was too weak to fight. Too ashamed of my failure to keep Eliza safe. It was my job."

"You were never weak," Tabitha said. "The evil that enthralled Eliza was powerful. She didn't know what had happened until it was too late."

Midnight crouched close. "We shouldn't stay much longer. We can talk later. Cut away those bindings. They're choking the life out of him."

"We can't cut them," Tabitha warned. "Not yet. They're laced with death magic. If we pull wrong, we'll tear Roland apart."

"Then we don't pull," I said. "We gently unravel and take as long as we need."

Midnight glanced over his shoulder. "I can only deceive Morticia for so long."

"I'll give her what for if she messes with us." Tabitha flattened her ears and hissed. "No one stops me from getting Roland back."

I pressed my head to Roland's once more, closed my eyes, and let the lingering threads of Eliza's magic rise in me.

Roland shuddered. "That's her! That's really her."

"Eliza left enough behind to finish this," I said.

The threads shifted, loosening their punishing grip. Roland wasn't free yet, but he would be, and we'd bring him home where he could heal.

***

The snow globe shimmered to life, Sage's voice tumbling through before her face even sharpened. "How's it going?"

279

"Roland is healing, but he's still a mess," I said. "Whiskers says he's a shadow of what he was. I don't think he even remembers how to be himself anymore, especially now it's sunk in that Eliza isn't coming back."

Sage sighed. "He's got time. He'll recover and find a new path. And he's not alone. Tabitha won't let him brood."

"And Midnight's got more compassion than he admits," I said. "As for Whiskers... I still don't trust him, but he hasn't put a paw wrong since we saved the village."

Sage's mouth quirked. "Are they your new magical misfits?"

I leaned closer to the globe. "You'll always be an original misfit. No one will replace you."

"That doesn't mean Roland wouldn't make an excellent member when he's ready."

"He is powerful," I admitted. "But it's hard seeing him so broken. Maybe he's endured too much and will simply fade."

"You've had your share of hard, Juno. Being banished, not seeing Zandra. Yet I don't see you fading."

"I'm not comparing."

"I am. You're stronger than you think. And more stubborn. That's what got you through this mystery. Not luck or borrowed spells."

"It takes a stubborn familiar to know one."

"Fair."

I hesitated, then confessed, "I'll tell you something, though. I miss it. My old magic was purrfection. This new stuff? It's like writing with the wrong paw."

"I wondered when you'd admit that," Sage said. "Your practice sessions have been... well, lacking."

"I'm still learning," I said. "It's just different. Everything feels wrong. Like the energy doesn't want to settle, and it doesn't truly belong to me."

"It hasn't grown into you," Sage said, studying me through the globe. "Or maybe you haven't grown into it. Give it time."

"Time. You love saying that."

"I'm ancient. I get to." She flicked an ear. "Have patience. And a nap. That always makes me feel better. When are you seeing Roland again?"

"In a few days. He's moving in with Tabitha. They've been spending a lot of time together."

"Trauma bonds," Sage murmured. "They share the pain of losing their witches and each other. Together, they can heal."

"I hope so. He's taking the lead on the memorial herb garden for Eliza. He liked the idea and said he wanted her to be remembered for her kindness. Before she got obsessed with the well, she used to gift herb bundles to villagers for good luck."

"That'll be good for him," Sage said. "Something positive to focus on. He'll make it with you around. Just remember, healing isn't linear. He could slide back. Make sure you're there to catch him."

I narrowed my eyes. "You and your wise phrases."

"You'd miss them if I stopped."

"Maybe. A little. But Roland doesn't need me. He has Tabitha and the others. I'm only staying because I have no choice."

"You may as well be comfortable while you're there," Sage said. "Accept their friendship. The library ghosts aren't enough to keep you out of trouble. Are the villagers still being friendly?"

"I got a half-smile from the baker. And Mrs. Kettleworth let me sit on the counter for a full minute before shooing me away," I said.

"It's progress," Sage said. "You'll soon have them eating out of your paw."

"They're cautious," I said. "And I get it. I'm a magical outsider with a habit of unearthing buried secrets and unleashing ancient evil. I wouldn't trust me, either."

"You solved a decades-old mystery and freed the village from magical control," Sage reminded me. "You're owed a thanks."

"I should suggest a statue in the center of the village, right next to the well. Which, by the way, is behaving beautifully."

Sage chuckled. "Don't push your luck. Go slowly. No one likes change."

"I guess," I said. "So... any word from Angel Force? They know what happened here, don't they?"

"They've heard," Sage replied. "I made sure of it. I sent the full recording of your actions to them in triplicate and marked it urgent."

"And?"

"They're intrigued but cautious. Finn wanted you to know he's fighting your corner."

I inhaled slowly. "But?"

"They're also slow to act. You know how the angels are."

"Bureaucracy with feathers," I muttered, "and reams of key performance indicators to meet. Where's the justice in that?"

"It's the higher angels who need convincing," Sage said with a sigh. "And we both know how flighty they are. We're doing everything we can to bring you home."

"I know you are." I blinked slowly, a cat's way of saying what my voice couldn't. "I just want to be with Zandra."

"She wants you here, too. We all do." Sage fell silent for a second. "While you wait, what are you planning to do?"

I gave a theatrical sigh. "Have a bottomless brunch of smoked salmon while perched on my witch's shoulder. But since I can't have either of those things, I want another case."

"I knew you'd say that! Have you found something interesting?"

"I just might." I leaned closer to the globe, lowering my voice. "It's weird and twisty. It involves an object that was meant to heal but ended up killing an empathetic healer. It sounds like it was hexed or cursed. Nasty."

"Are you sure you don't want something less deadly?"

"I just stopped an ancient spider-like evil from opening a lethal portal and helped to unbury a magical soul-tied familiar from a cursed grave. I can handle anything."

"Well, alright then," Sage said, her eyes glimmering through the glass. "You pull the hex file, and let's solve our next cold case."

Afterword

I hope you loved reading The Case of the Whispering Well as much as I loved writing it.

Book two, The Case of the Hexed Heart, is available now.

Here's a little blurb to get you in the mood.

Can a banished magical cat solve the cold case that baffled everyone?

When a respected magical healer is found dead in Badger's Haze's long-abandoned observatory wing, heart stopped, mouth agape, and a cursed brooch clutched in her hand, the case is quietly buried by Angel Force when they fail to find the killer.

Decades later, the file has resurfaced. And there's only one magical cat with the claws (and curiosity) to sniff out the truth.

Banished familiar Juno, still stuck living in the haunted village library and communicating with fellow cat Sage through a temperamental snow globe, dives into a web of magical secrets, old rivalries, and deadly enchantments. The brooch—known as the Hexed Heart—is misfiring across the village. And something is stirring. Something dangerous.

Add in suspects (all magical, all with motive), a blind-in-one-eye cat, and a growing storm of misfiring magic, and Juno is about to face her most baffling case yet.

Solving this paranormal cold case could be the key to her freedom. If it doesn't kill her first.

Get your copy of The Hexed Heart in ebook or paperback.

About the author

K.E. O'Connor (Karen) is a cozy mystery author living in the beautiful British countryside. She loves all things mystery, animals, and cake.

When she's not writing, she volunteers at a local animal sanctuary, reads a ton of books, binge watches mystery series, and dreams of living somewhere warmer.

To stay in touch with the mysteries, where the killer always gets caught, justice is served magic style, and the familiars talk, join her newsletter.

Newsletter:
www.subscribepage.com/cozymysteries
Website: www.keoconnor.com
Facebook: www.facebook.com/keoconnorauthor

www.ingramcontent.com/pod-product-compliance
Lightning Source LLC
Chambersburg PA
CBHW050557190726
48283CB00007B/2180